The Mystery of Ghost Canyon

Bret King Mystery Stories

BY DAN SCOTT

Bret's flashlight suddenly gleamed on a blanched skull

A BRET KING MYSTERY

The Mystery of Ghost Canyon

By DAN SCOTT

Illustrated by JOE BEELER

Grosset & Dunlap PUBLISHERS

NEW YORK

Contents

The Mystery of Ghost Canyon

CHAPTER I

Mysterious Tracks

BRET KING sat straight in the saddle, gazing over the rugged New Mexico range. Just eighteen, he was man-tall and cowboy-lean, his father's mainstay on Rimrock Ranch. His blue eyes now looked perplexed.

"We've tallied eight hundred and sixty-three head, boys." Bret spoke soberly to three other young riders reined up beside him. "And we've combed this pasture clean. It means Rimrock is short twenty valuable yearling steers."

"Too many!" said Benny Ortega. His dark, round face looked somber.

Ace Tallchief merely nodded, while Vic Martinson used a silk bandanna to wipe the dust from his glasses.

Suddenly Bret exclaimed, "Benny! Don't let your horse move! There's a rattler under that mesquite bush to your right!"

1

In a flash both Bret and Ace were off their horses, making double-end flails of their ropes to kill the snake. But it did not move.

"Already dead! Shot!" exclaimed Ace, never one to waste words. Then he pointed. "Look! Man track. But no cowboy boots. Flat shoes."

"Somebody trespassing where they've got no business," Bret said grimly.

For a moment the four companions remained silent in thought. Benny, nineteen, a Rimrock cowboy of New Mexican Spanish ancestry, coiled his lariat. He glanced at Ace, whose appaloosa pawed at a passing tumbleweed. Ace, a boyhood schoolmate of Bret, was a Navajo and possessed the inborn range wisdom of his people. Although he lived in Tovar with his father, the Indian kept his horse at the Rimrock, where he was considered part of the King family.

Vic was the son of Tovar's bank president and a newcomer to the West. He was seventeen, handsome, and studious. As Bret put it, Vic did not "savvy cow," but the boys all liked him just the same.

Thoughtfully Bret pushed the gray cowboy sombrero halfway back on his brown hair. "I figure rustlers would work on horseback. Let's look around."

Bret paused, winked at Vic, and picked up a long stick. He lifted the dead snake and tossed it toward Benny's saddle.

"Here's your rattler, Benny." Bret grinned. "Want to skin him for a hatband?"

With a snort Benny's horse jumped six feet sideways, nearly unseating the rider.

"Well, gee my wheeze!" Benny's grin was white-toothed and wide. "If you got me thrown off, I'd tie snake around you for a necktie!"

"You cowboys certainly play rough!" exclaimed Vic.

"Sometimes we have to," said Bret. "So we try to keep in practice."

"On Rimrock Ranch, no cowboys ride," sang out Benny Ortega, who liked to make rhymes, "if they ain't made of tough rawhide!"

"Never mind the poetry, Shorty," Bret said quickly. "Let's spread out to find where this flat-footed track came from."

"Just a minute!" Benny called. He spurred his jittery horse alongside the dead rattler, leaned from the saddle, picked up the snake in one long reach, and tied it on behind his saddle. "Make nice hatband. Maybe I get Jinx to skin for me."

"More likely she'll skin *you* if you get playful with that snake," said Bret. "Come on. Let's get going!"

Jinx, short for Jennifer, was Bret's sixteen-year-old sister. Saddlewise as any cowboy, she had killed many a rattlesnake, but would never touch one.

Spreading out to cover more ground, the boys

began their search for additional rustler signs.

It was Bret's range-trained eyes that spotted tire tracks. The companions quickly dismounted.

"They don't look like any tires we use on the ranch," said Bret. "But I'm not dead sure."

Swiftly Ace's slim brown hands smoothed out a spot of sand. With a twig he drew the perfect pattern of a tire tread.

"This is the tire track of the Rimrock pickup truck," he declared. "This other one is not the same."

Vic looked on admiringly. "Ace, you're a real artist. Where'd you learn to draw?"

"It is the ancient art of the Navajo to make pictures in sand," Ace replied modestly.

"You should visit his father's shop in Tovar, Vic," Bret said. "Fine silverwork, sketches, paintings—"

"Hey! Look yonder!" Benny broke in excitedly. "It's Rusty—in much big hurry!"

Rusty was Bret's twelve-year-old, red-haired, impish brother. He had a special hobby of raising Shetland ponies. Now he came riding one of them down the hill as fast as the short-legged pony could carry him.

About five yards away, the Shetland's front hoof hit a gopher hole. Down he went, end for end. Rusty sailed off over his head. He landed in a rolling somersault that brought him up unhurt and on his feet in front of Bret.

"We'd better rent you out to a circus," Bret remarked dryly. "You got Indians after you, or what?"

Rusty shook his head. His big gray-blue eyes were wide with excitement.

"I've found something, Bret!" he panted. "Over in Coyote Cove right at the foot of the Rimrock Mesa. Come on and look!"

Benny shrugged. "Why you don't tell us what is it?"

"It—it's something important—I think!" Rusty managed to look mysterious. "Just come look and see if it isn't, Bret!"

This could be one of Rusty's practical jokes, but Bret did not think so—not with Rusty riding one of his precious Shetlands that fast and all asweat with excitement.

"All right, Paul Revere," Bret said with a slap on the back. "We'll take a look. First let's see if Chopo's hurt. If he's too crippled to carry you, maybe you can carry *him*."

Rusty grinned. He was used to Bret's banter about the size of "Rusty's midget mustangs."

The Shetland, thanks partly to the softness of the gopher's workings, and partly to his own sturdy chunkiness, had suffered no injury.

As soon as the little horse had caught his wind, Rusty adjusted the saddle cinch and mounted him. The other four mounted their horses and all struck out at a lope westward toward Rimrock Mesa, a tawny, knife-edged mass of rock from which the ranch took its name.

Crossing sparsely grassed Sacaton Draw on the way, Vic, who was in the rear, suddenly reined up.

"Look, Bret!" he called, pointing off to the left. "More tire tracks!"

Bret and the others whirled quickly and rode to look at them. The tracks were clear this time, and of the same tread they had seen before.

"You've got sharp eyes, Vic," said Bret. "I would have missed them. Just goes to show that when you're going fast, sometimes you fail to notice important things."

Vic looked pleased at the compliment.

"Maybe these tracks have something to do with what Rusty wants to show us," he suggested. "Do they, Rusty?"

Rusty sailed over Chopo's head

"I don't know," Rusty mused. "I want Bret to look first, before I make any guesses."

"Rusty," Bret said soberly, "I can find whatever it is you want us to see. I wish you'd ride on home to the ranch."

"Gosh, Bret! I don't want to!"

"Strange tire tracks aren't all we've found, Rusty," Bret explained. "Somebody shot a rattler back yonder. There's skulduggery afoot. If it's rustlers with guns—and we run onto them—well, I'd rather you were safe at home."

Rusty looked up at the brother he idolized. "I'll go if you say so, Bret." He grinned impishly. "But I warn you—I'm liable to tell Mom a pretty wild story."

"All right, then." Bret laughed. "Come along. If rustlers shoot at us, we'll do the running while you throw rocks at 'em!"

"That suits me, too," Benny said. "Whenever there's fighting with rustlers to do, Benny Ortega will leave it to you."

Although they did not come on any rustlers, what Rusty had to show them did not ease Bret's mind. Rusty pointed to a hole in the ground well hidden by surrounding juniper and piñon trees. It was bigger than a badger hole and about two feet deep.

"Wow!" exclaimed Vic. "Some animal is certainly quite a digger!"

"Coyote," said Ace. "He smelled something and dug."

"Right," Bret agreed. "And whatever he dug up was buried by a man. There's some more of the same shoe prints we saw back yonder."

"Look!" put in Rusty, reading a fresh clue in the dusty earth. "Something has been dragged off. I'll bet it was a steer hide."

"I'll follow the drag," Benny offered, "and see what I can find."

"Go ahead," Bret told him. "I'm going to play badger and dig deeper into this hole."

When Benny returned a few minutes later with fragments of chewed steer hide, Bret already had the result of his digging spread out on the ground —a fairly fresh steer hide. The brand on it was RK, the mark of the Rimrock Ranch.

"Well, gee my wheeze!" Benny exclaimed. "What do you know about that!"

"Truck rustlers are working the Rimrock—for the first time—but not likely for the last," Bret said grimly.

"I've read about truck rustlers," Vic ventured. "They slip in at night, shoot a few steers, then either load them whole in the truck or skin them and bury the hides. They race to a highway with the stolen beef, then sell it—maybe two hundred miles away."

"And who can track a truck on a blacktop

highway?" Bret said bitterly. "It's worse than old-time rustling." He rolled up the steer hide.

"I can tell you one thing, boys," Bret continued between tight lips. "They won't get away with it long on the Rimrock—not if I have to ride day and night to catch them."

"You won't have to ride alone," Benny promised, and the others echoed their agreement.

"I'll take this hide in," Bret stated. "We may need it for evidence."

Bret approached Kiote, his favorite cow horse. A quarter-horse type, he was a buckskin dun with black mane and tail and a dark stripe down his back—the color cowboys call *bayo coyote*. Hence Bret had named him "Kiote."

But no sooner had the cowboy hit the saddle with the steer hide under one arm than Kiote, frightened by the smell, lunged into a frantic spell of pitching.

"Ride 'em, Bret!" Rusty shouted, thoroughly enjoying the performance.

But salty rider though he was, Bret suddenly lost his seat and sailed through the air.

CHAPTER II

Missing Cowboy

Vic gasped as Bret landed hard. But he rolled with the fall and came up with nothing more than a limp. Smiling wryly, Bret reached for the reins of his jittery mount.

"Wait!" said Ace. "I'll show you." He smeared his hands on the hide, then rubbed them all over his horse's nostrils.

"Indian trick," he said, with one of his rare grins. "Now *everything* smells like steer hide. He doesn't know where it comes from, so he's not afraid."

Ace swung the hide across his saddle and mounted. The horse snorted, but that was all.

"Ace"—grinned Bret, as they headed for the ranch—"I'm glad you keep your horse here. Both of you could come in right handy before this rustling ruckus is over!"

It was nearing noon when the boys reached Rimrock Ranch with their ominous news. They halted at the corrals. These were a long cluster of adjoining stock pens, the nearest some fifty yards from the house across a graveled area, wide open except for a watering trough at one end.

The corral fences, about six feet high, were built of stout, horizontal two-by-eights, with about five-inch cracks between the boards.

Adjoining the corrals on the side away from the house was an irregular line of stables, hay sheds, tool sheds, saddle sheds, and other outbuildings. Some were of adobe, others of lumber, but all had pitched roofs for the easy shedding of winter snow.

At the west end of these loomed a huge round water tank set on top of a stone-walled pump house. At the east end was a small pen around the cattle-weighing scales, with a ramp and loading chute just back of it. Off a few yards farther east stood the long, low adobe bunkhouse.

Taken altogether, corrals and buildings formed a crescent facing the main house. Painted a warm dark red, they presented a pleasing picture as well as a neat example of modern stock-handling efficiency.

In the horse corral a tall, strapping, middle-aged man and slender girl were doctoring a young horse's wire-cut leg.

James J. King, the boss of Rimrock Ranch,

was called "Big Jim" by everybody, whether in affection, respect, or downright awe.

The girl was Jinx, pretty, with laughing hazel eyes, curly auburn hair, and a smile dimple. It showed as she greeted Bret with a nod.

Stepping off his horse to help hold the colt, Bret saw that his father's face was flushed with anger.

"Not a foot of loose wire on the place," Big Jim growled, "but some crazy rock hunter breaks down a wire gate to let his car through and a fine colt gets cut bad!"

Bret waited till the doctoring was finished, then said gravely, "I'm afraid it wasn't just a geologist, Dad. Come look at the steer hide we dug up. We found tracks, too!"

Vic and Jinx stayed to quiet the colt while Big Jim went to examine the hide. His face was grim as he looked at it.

"I found where they buried it," Rusty said with pride.

"Good boy." Big Jim patted his shoulder, then stood silent a moment. A flinty look came into his eyes.

"Truck rustlers," he said grimly. "Our New Mexico Cattlemen's Association has been after them farther south, even offering big rewards, without much luck. But if the low-down thieves think they can get away with it on the RK, they've got another think coming!"

"We'll catch them, Dad," Bret told him. "Ace and Benny and Vic are all ready to help."

"Me too!" Rusty exclaimed.

"Sure." Big Jim nodded. "But we'd better phone Sheriff Buxton. Let's hang this hide on the fence to dry. We may need it in court."

While Benny hung up the hide, the others unsaddled and turned the horses into the feed corral.

Bret, meantime, told his father about the other clues they had found, and added, "I'll bet the tire tracks at the open gate match the ones we saw."

"Likely," Big Jim agreed. "We'll check."

Ace, squatting on his heels, smoothed a spot on the ground. With incredible ease he drew a tire-tread pattern. "The tracks we found are like this," he explained.

Big Jim studied the tread, then shook his head. "Not like the ones at the gate. But it could be the same people using different trucks. We'd better phone Buxton."

As they strode toward the house, a musical *clink-clank* sounded from the doorway. Mrs. King was tapping a steel triangle calling them to noontime dinner.

Hope Chandler King was a slim, dark-haired, vivacious former schoolteacher from New England. But she had readily adopted cow-country customs after marrying Big Jim. She rang again, and everybody came running.

Big Jim studied the tire-tread pattern

"Race you to the front gate, Sis!" Rusty challenged Jinx. The girl ran as gracefully as an antelope. Rusty's gait, although speedy, was more like the gallop of a pony. The race would have been even, if Benny had not grabbed Rusty's shirttail as he passed.

"Shame on you!" Jinx scolded the cowboy. "You spoiled the race."

Turning, she tugged Benny's dusty black hat down over his eyes in high-spirited good humor.

The main house was a long adobe, shaped like an open E. A vine-shaded porch ran its full length. Four huge cottonwoods stood in the green, picket-fenced yard like giant sentinels on guard.

"Everybody hurry up and wash." Mrs. King smiled at them from the door. "Dinner's on." Then she saw the set look on Big Jim's face and quickly asked him what was the matter.

"Rustlers," he told her. "Excuse Bret and me while we phone Sheriff Buxton."

At the telephone in the hallway Big Jim let Bret do the talking. It was the sheriff's eighteen-year-old son, Andy, who answered. Young Buxton, a transplanted Texan, was a close friend of Bret. When Andy said the sheriff was out, Bret explained the situation.

"Don't worry!" came Andy's slow drawl. "Back in Texas we used to catch New Mexican rustlers in mousetraps!"

"Andy! This is serious!"

"Okay, Bret, don't bust a cinch. I'll get Dad right away."

Bret and Big Jim were last to be seated at the well-spread table. Mrs. King was used to hearty appetites and welcomed young guests. Juicy roast beef, pinto beans, hot biscuits, and gravy were plentiful. And her big apple pies were cut four ways instead of six.

While they ate, Big Jim and Bret recounted the story of the truck rustlers.

"We'll trail them as soon as Buxton arrives," Big Jim said.

"I'm glad you called the sheriff," Mrs. King said. "I don't want any of my boys getting hurt."

"Shucks, Mom," Rusty said scornfully, "we aren't afraid of any old rustlers!"

"My favorite wrangler"—she gave his hair a rub—"will stay home to take care of his mom."

"Aw gee!" Rusty protested. "I'm the one who found where they buried the hide!"

"You know who's boss around here," Big Jim said, smiling for the first time in the past hour.

Mrs. King's laughter was a relief from the tension they were all feeling.

"May I go along, Dad—at least this afternoon?" Jinx asked. "I could hold the horses in case you have to sneak up on the rustlers."

"Well, now—" Big Jim hesitated, then patted

her hand. "All right—for this afternoon. Right now I wish you and Benny would run in some fresh horses."

"I'll help, too," Vic offered.

"Old Vic," Rusty chortled. "He always wants to go wherever Jinx goes. Hah!"

For answer to that, Jinx pulled out his shirttail as she went past.

By the time fresh horses were corralled, Andy Buxton had arrived on his motorcycle from Tovar, ten miles distant.

"Gee my wheeze!" said Benny, imitating Andy's drawl. "I don't think we got a saddle to fit that kind of horse!"

"Texans ride everything from alligators to cyclones." The husky youth grinned, wiping sweat from his crew cut. He motioned with his thumb. "Dad's coming."

A minute later Sheriff Buxton arrived in his official car, high-wheeled for rough roads. Buxton was a lean man with a strong-jawed face, a little gray in his strawish hair.

Quickly Big Jim briefed him about the trouble. Ace supplied drawings of the suspicious tire tracks, and Bret brought the steer hide for the sheriff to examine.

"We'll scout," Sheriff Buxton said tersely. "If you're all saddled up, let's go!"

"Wait!" Bret exclaimed suddenly. "I've found something!"

With his pocketknife he dug a mushroomed, soft-nosed bullet from the thick neck skin of the steer hide.

"Looks like a .38," said the sheriff. "Could turn out to be evidence. I'll keep it."

He put the slug in his pocket and they all left the ranch as one party, to spread out later. Big Jim rode with Buxton in the sheriff's car, the rest went on horseback.

Jinx, in blue jeans like the boys, rode Silky, her favorite palomino—the one she used for learning trick riding. But there was no frolicking today. This excursion was serious, and they knew it.

Half a mile from the house the party split up. The car followed a roundabout route. The riders took a shorter trail too rough for car travel. They met again in Sacaton Draw, where the boys had found the suspicious tire tracks.

"Who's the best tracker?" the sheriff asked.

"Ace could track a bee in a blizzard," Bret told him. "Let him go with you and Dad. The rest of us will spread out and see what we can find."

Riding ahead of the car, the young Navajo had no trouble following the tire tracks. The others dispersed to cover more country.

Jinx had ridden several miles, traveling in a great arc, when she topped a rise and stopped to scan the cactus-studded range. Far in the distance she saw Bret and Andy, dismounted. They seemed to be mending a broken gate.

Suddenly Jinx's palomino snorted and shied. "Another pesky snake," Jinx thought. She dismounted, holding her lariat in readiness. But what she found was a wadded steer hide under a pile of rocks. She left it and hurried to the boys.

"Those rustlers must have made a big haul," Bret said when she told him. "They probably cut the fence here to come in."

As soon as the boys finished mending the break, the trio rode back to pick up the hide and "read sign," as cowboys say. But the area was too rocky for tracks to show.

It was after sundown when they all met the sheriff's car. All, that is, except Benny.

"Where's Ortega?" the sheriff asked.

Big Jim replied, "I gave him leave this morning to ride to Oro Perdido Canyon. He wants to see how his folks are. He's coming back later tonight." He turned to the others. "Did any of you kids find anything?"

Bret told about the gate and the steer hide. Then Vic reported, "Benny and I saw a steer with a bloody spot on the loose neck skin, as if perhaps it had been shot. I thought we should drive it in, but Benny said it wasn't hurt badly enough to need doctoring."

Buxton growled disdainfully. "Even shooting close up with a spotlight sometimes they miss. Well, here's what we found: the truck tracks crossed an arroyo my car couldn't navigate. So we followed on foot. The tracks turned into the main graveled road toward town."

"Do you think truck rustlers could sell stolen beef in Tovar?" Bret asked.

Buxton thought for a moment. "Possible. There's a new butcher shop—man named Otto Mueller runs it. We'll have to check on him."

"Do you think we'd better ride the steer pastures tonight, Sheriff?" Bret asked.

Big Jim answered, "That's what we've already decided. We'll get fresh horses. The sheriff will ride till midnight, then I'll take over."

"Hold on here!" Bret exclaimed. "What about the rest of us?"

"I won't ask my son or anybody else to risk getting shot," Big Jim said firmly. "Besides—"

"What you risk, we risk, Dad."

Ace, Andy, Vic, and Jinx all nodded vigorous agreement.

"Pretty sassy, aren't you?" There was pride in Big Jim's eyes. "Well—all right—except for Jinx. Her mother would have my hide!"

Jinx was not happy about the decision and her frown showed it. But when Big Jim grinned at her, Jinx's dimpled smile returned.

They rode the steer pastures in two shifts that night, shadowy and silent in the darkness, watching, listening. Nothing happened.

But at midnight Benny Ortega had not returned to the RK.

"It's not like Benny to be late," said Bret, who was riding beside his father.

"He might have misunderstood. Benny will be here at sunup."

The next morning the faithful cowboy was still missing from the bunkhouse.

"Something's happened," Bret said worriedly, as the family finished breakfast.

"Perhaps one of Benny's parents is ill," Mrs. King ventured. "Bret, why don't you and Rusty ride to Oro Perdido and see?"

"The rest of us will be on the lookout for him, too," Big Jim said. "The first one to find Benny will send a smoke signal from the mesa. Agreed?"

"Okay, Dad."

The brothers mounted and rode silently toward the Ortega sheep ranch, which adjoined the King spread. Skirting the base of Rimrock Mesa, they approached the fold in a rocky hillside which led into Oro Perdido Canyon.

"This place always seemed spooky to me," Rusty said.

Bret half smiled. "I know what you mean. I never did much like exploring here, either. The Spanish spin wild tales about Oro Perdido."

The boys descended into a long, narrow canyon. At the far end, two ragged tufa cliffs pinched off the exit. But the canyon floor, watered by a small stream, was green with grass, on which a flock of sheep and a few goats grazed.

Off to the left, under the shelter of the rock wall, stood a simple three-room adobe house. The window casings of the humble dwelling were painted turquoise blue. Above them, through the neatly mud-plastered wall, protruded the ends of log roof beams. And from these *vegas* hung strings of bright red chilies.

Benny's horse stood before the open door.

Bret's frown vanished. Smiling, he turned to Rusty. "Anyway, Benny is—"

The boy's remark was cut off by a woman who ran from the house. "Señor Bret!" she cried out. "Benny's horse come home, but no Benny. Where is he?"

CHAPTER III

Ghost Talk

SHOCKED by Mrs. Ortega's outcry, Bret and Rusty rode up quickly and dismounted. Benny's mother, a plump, pleasant-faced woman, was not hysterical, but tears in her eyes betrayed her intense anxiety.

"My poor Benedito!" she kept crying in Spanish. "The only one we have left at home—my youngest —and now we have lost him."

Just then her husband, a stooped, slender man, hurried from the house to her side.

"Hush, Mela!" Don Miguel Ortega scolded her. "Benny's friends will find him. Do you think somebody hurt my son, Señor Bret?"

"Most certainly not," Bret assured him in the Spanish he had spoken from childhood.

Bret, nonetheless, was heartsick with the same thought—or worse, that possibly the young cowboy had been shot by intruders on the RK.

"Was there nothing, no clues on the horse or saddle, Don Miguel?" Bret asked anxiously.

"Nothing, son." Don Miguel shook his gray head. "But there was no blood, either."

"I'll bet Benny caught a rustler," Rusty offered with enthusiasm. "Probably got him tied down and has to stay with him so he won't get loose."

"Could be," Bret agreed, trying to sound hopeful. "Anyhow, our best bet is to backtrack his horse—if we can."

He turned to lay a comforting hand on Mrs. Ortega's shoulder and quickly explained the rustling trouble. "The folks at the ranch are looking for Benny, too, Doña Mela. Maybe they have already found him. If they haven't, I promise you, Rusty and I will."

"Good boy!" said Mrs. Ortega. *"Vaya con Dios. Go with God!"*

"My herder, my dog, and my only two horses are out with my sheep," Mr. Ortega said. "And I am lame of the leg. But I also will go where I can to search."

He followed Bret and Rusty out to their horses.

"It's agreed between us and those at the ranch," Bret told him, "to send a smoke signal from the mesa when Benny is found. I didn't mention this to Doña Mela, because so far there has been no smoke."

"Understood," said Mr. Ortega.

"We'll lead Benny's horse," Bret told Rusty as

they set out. "We'll need it whether we find Benny alive or dead."

"We've got to find him alive, Bret!" Rusty was not far from tears. *"We've got to!"*

"Sure, Rusty." Bret gave the boy a reassuring whack on the shoulder. "Let's go!"

Backtracking Benny's horse was not easy. The animal had stopped here and there to graze and meander. Also, there were rocky places where even a shod horse made little or no track.

Finally, circling around the foot of Rimrock Mesa, the boys came to a dim old Indian trail that no one ever used. It was narrow, rocky, and tortuous, climbing steeply up toward the mesa's rim. In it were fresh tracks of a horse wearing a number-one shoe. The tracks went both ways, but those descending proved to be on top.

"It's Benny's horse all right," Bret said. "But why would he be riding up here?"

The climb was hard, but it paid off. Halfway up the mesa they met Benny, staggering down the trail. He wore a dazed look.

"Benny! What happened?" Bret exclaimed.

Benny took a long drink of water from the small canteen Bret offered him. "I was riding around the mesa," he told them, "when I saw a flash up on the rim—like somebody signaling with a looking glass. So I say to myself: 'Benny, you better find out about this.' I am high up under the rim when a rock hit me on top the head, knock me off my horse, unconscious, so that only now I am able to get up and walk. Maybe just a falling rock. Maybe—"

"More likely somebody threw it from above," Bret broke in. "Anyhow, you're safe! Here, let me help you on your horse."

"Well, gee my wheeze!" Benny grinned. "This the first time I ever need help to get on a horse, *amigo!*"

"Of course if you don't feel able to ride yet—" Bret began, but Benny laughed.

"When a cowboy doesn't feel able to ride," he

declared, "that's because somebody chopped off his head and hid it from him!"

As they jogged back down the steep trail, Rusty asked curiously, "Where does this old trail go, Benny?"

"One fork climbs the mesa." Benny pointed. "The other circles under the rim to prehistoric cliff dwellings. Some call it *'La Cueva del Oro Perdido'*—'Cave of the Lost Gold.' But I call it *'La Cueva de los Chisos'*—'Cave of the Ghosts.' A good place to stay away from!"

"Why?" insisted Rusty. "Do you really think there are ghosts up there?"

Instead of answering, Benny ruefully felt the bump on his head, then began to sing:

> *"I'd like to be a coyote,*
> *He run, he jump, he walk,*
> *He catch some mice, but what is nice,*
> *He never have to talk!"*

"Aw, shucks!" Rusty complained, but try as he might, he could not get Benny to talk about the cliff dwellers' cave. However, Benny did point it out to them as they topped the low ridge over into Oro Perdido Canyon.

As they approached the Ortega place, Benny dismounted and hallooed. His parents rushed out, waving their arms.

"My poor little Benedito!" cried Mrs. Ortega,

hugging the boy tightly. But this time her tears were tears of joy.

"Unsaddle your horses," urged Don Miguel. "I will feed them hay."

"And I will feed my heroes better than that!" Doña Mela smiled hospitably.

Hardly had Bret accepted the invitation in the proper Spanish phrases when Ace and Vic rode in from another direction. Andy Buxton and his father, they reported, had been called to Tovar.

"Well, we didn't have the honor of finding Benny," Vic reported. "But we did discover something—tracks of a ridden horse. They came from the direction of the Flying Spur Ranch and went back the same way." He motioned toward the far side of the Rimrock Ranch where the expansive Flying Spur bordered the King land.

"More trespassers!" Bret exclaimed. "Or maybe just a cowboy after a stray."

"No tracks of driving a cow," Ace reported.

The boys' discussion of this new mystery was interrupted by Mrs. Ortega, asking Benny to invite the others to dinner.

"Our house is poor," Benny said in English, with the typical spreading of hands that is a Spanish gesture of hospitality. "But it is yours." Then he grinned and added, "Mamá is a fine cook, too!"

"*Gracias!*" said Vic, having learned the Spanish word for "thank you."

"I almost forgot, folks," Bret said suddenly.

"I've got to make a signal fire on the mesa, so the RK will know Benny has been found."

"I go," Ace offered. "My Boojum climb quick." The Navajo picked up a shovel and struck out up a steep trail on his stout appaloosa.

"Why did he take a shovel?" Vic asked.

"He'll have to put out his signal fire with earth," Bret exclaimed. "No water on the mesa."

"Gosh," sighed Rusty, "I hope some old ghost doesn't drop a rock on Ace's head, too!"

While Mrs. Ortega went inside to prepare dinner, Don Miguel showed the boys his garden; mostly corn, beans, squashes, and chilies. As the boys strolled back toward the house they saw a column of dense smoke rising from a high point on the mesa.

"Little fire, big smoke," Bret commented. "The Indians know how."

Ace was not back yet when Mrs. Ortega called them to the table, but a place was saved for him on one of the kitchen benches that served as chairs. Ace came in soon after Don Miguel had said grace.

Vic, the only one who felt strange in these surroundings, glanced curiously about the neat interior. The whitewashed walls were adorned with framed lithographs of the Virgin Mary and various saints. Over each frame hung a garland of handmade white lace. Bret saw how much Vic admired it all, and that pleased him, for the Ortegas were dear friends.

As was the custom of her people, Doña Mela did not sit down with her male guests. She hovered about, happily serving coffee for Don Miguel, fresh goat's milk for the others.

While they ate, Benny and Don Miguel told Vic the Southwest Spanish names for the various dishes. The meat was *cabrito*—young kid, succulent and tender, swimming in a sauce of red chili.

Bret took a generous helping from a big bowl. *"Frijoles,"* he said. "Pinto beans, the mainstay of life in New Mexico."

Don Miguel passed a plate of thick, unleavened pancakes. "You like our *tortillas?"*

"We like!" said Vic, helping himself to a salad of wild watercress. "And what is this?"

Benny smiled. *"Berro.* And don't forget you roll the r's. And this bowl is *posole"*—he pointed—"Mexican hominy made of blue corn."

"Navajos make the same with red corn," Ace said. "All Indians like bright-color corn."

"I'll bet even ghosts would go for Doña Mela's cooking," Rusty said, blinking back tears from a swallow of red-hot chili.

For dessert, Mrs. Ortega served fried tarts filled with dried apricots.

"A real feast, Doña Mela," said Bret in Spanish. "Thanks to you—and God. Now we must get back to the ranch."

"Please come again," she said shyly in English. "Always wel-come!"

Joining his companions, Benny mounted, and the boys rode off.

Halfway back to the Rimrock Ranch, Bret saw a big dust cloud swiftly coming toward them. It was Andy Buxton in a bouncing Rimrock pickup truck. A few minutes later Andy hit the brakes hard, screeching to a stop near the horses. He shouted through the window.

"Fellows! I've got big news!"

CHAPTER IV

A Suspect

"BIG news?" Bret grinned. "I suppose Texas slid into the Gulf of Mexico and got lost!"

"Never mind the wisecracks, cowboy!" Andy retorted. "Ballistics tests show that the bullet you dug out of that yearling's hide was shot from the same gun that rustlers used to kill a steer up in Wyoming three weeks ago."

"Wyoming! Those crooks get around. I'm afraid that we're up against something big, Andy—big, well-organized, and plenty tough."

Briefly, Bret told Andy about Benny's narrow escape, possibly from an unknown assailant, and Benny displayed the knob on his head.

"Texas hummingbirds lay bigger eggs than that," quipped young Buxton. Then promptly sober again, he added, "You got any ideas, Bret?"

"Benny knows a place where there are ghosts," put in Rusty. "It's a cliff dwelling. I'll bet—"

"Ghosts don't butcher steers, buster," Bret interrupted dryly. "Boys, the way I look at it, all this riding we've done will scare off any truck rustlers for at least a day or two. Right?"

"It seems logical," Vic agreed, and the others nodded.

"All right," Bret went on. "Ace has some designing work to do at his father's shop, and Vic tells me he must run some errands for his dad at the bank. Benny and Dad can hold down the ranch, while Andy and I drive into Tovar in the morning to scout for clues to the rustlers."

"What about me?" Rusty asked.

"You can put in the day teaching your midget mustangs to walk on stilts," Bret teased Rusty good-humoredly, "or go hunt ghosts, whichever you'd rather."

"Aw, shucks!" said Rusty. But he made no further protest. To the twelve-year-old, his tall brother was what cowboys call "the main high horny toad," to be looked up to and obeyed.

"That's settled then," Bret said. "Andy, can you think of anyone in Tovar who might be mixed up in this?"

"Nobody but that new butcher, Otto Mueller."

"We'll look him over and see if we can read his brand," said Bret. "You can stay the night with us, Andy—if you'll promise not to talk about Texas. We'll meet you at the ranch."

That evening after supper Benny got out his battered old guitar. They all sat on the pleasant *portal* and sang old cowboy songs.

"This is the life!" said Vic, and Jinx gave him a smile. But the shadow of the truck rustler mystery still lurked in the minds of all of them. Even when they laughed at Benny's comic rendition of the Mexican cockroach song "La Cucaracha," Bret's thoughts were on the chore he had set for himself and Andy in Tovar the next day.

At nine o'clock that Wednesday morning the modest ranch-country town of Tovar looked as quiet and peaceful as an old cow chewing her cud.

Bret dropped Ace where a sign said ASA TALL-CHIEF—NAVAJO ARTS AND CRAFTS, and let Vic off at the Stockmen's Bank. Then he and Andy wasted no time getting to Otto Mueller's small butcher shop on a side street.

Mueller, short, stout, and flaxen-haired, was alone, slicing pork chops when they came in.

"Something I can do for you, gentlemen?" Mueller asked, not stopping his work.

"We're thinking of putting in a new freezer locker at the ranch," Bret said politely. "We'd like to look at yours and see how it works."

"*Ach!*" Mueller looked up with a scowl. "I got no time to show lockers!"

Bret and Andy exchanged significant glances. The butcher's refusal had aroused their suspicions.

"I believe you're new here," drawled Andy casually. "I'm Sheriff Buxton's meat-loving son. This is my friend, Bret King, of Rimrock Ranch. I'll take a dozen of those nice pork chops."

"In that case"—Mueller shrugged grumpily—"there's the freeze room. Walk in. Make yourselves at home."

"Thank you," Bret said. He swung the heavily insulated door open and they walked in.

"Boy, this is sure 'nuff cold!" Andy shivered as the door clicked shut behind the boys. "Hey! How do we get out of here?"

Andy tried the door lever—and found it locked. Bret tried it, with the same result. Through a small frosty window they saw the round pink face of Otto Mueller laughing at them.

"Andy," Bret said in a strangely quiet tone, "we're in a fix. If this butcher is in cahoots with the rustlers, he's got us trapped. We'll freeze to death in here!"

"And I'll never see Texas again!" Andy tried to sound jovial, but his eyes held a look of fear.

Suddenly Bret exclaimed, "Andy! There's only one beef carcass in here. It's got too much tallow for a range steer and it's been aged too long to be RK beef."

"We're locked in just the same," Andy replied glumly. "And if we don't get out soon—"

He broke off suddenly. Outside the little window, Otto Mueller was motioning to them, pointing toward a button they had not noticed. Bret pushed it and the big door swung open.

"Dummkopfs!" The fat butcher chuckled. "Before you go into any place, you should know how you're going to get out, *nein?"*

"That makes sense," Bret said, and he and Andy joined Mueller in laughing at their carelessness.

For a few minutes they chatted with Mueller, telling him what a nice place he had. Then Bret decided to lay their cards on the table.

"We're on the trail of beef thieves, Mr. Mueller," he said, "and you can help us. Has anybody offered to sell you fresh beef lately?"

Mueller took time to scratch his chin.

"*Yah,*" he said finally. "Last week, a stranger— rough-looking fellow with black whiskers—like for a week he don't shave. He was driving a dark-green truck—maybe about one-ton pickup."

"Did you notice anything special besides his whiskers?" Andy asked. "Did he have on boots or flat shoes?"

"His feet I did not notice," Mueller told them, "but his mouth— It was big, like this—" He stuck two fingers in his mouth and pulled the corners of it almost back to his ears. "He priced the beef enough cheap, but his looks I did not like. So I told him I need no beef."

"Thanks, Mr. Mueller," Bret said warmly. "This may be just the clue we're looking for. Was he alone in the truck?"

"Yah, I think so, unless somebody was hiding in the back. It was covered with a wagon sheet."

"Did you see which way the truck went?" Andy asked, but to that Mueller shook his head.

Bret thanked the butcher again, Andy paid for his package of pork chops, and they went out to the street.

"Dark-green pickup, a rough-looking character, black whiskers, wide mouth—not too much to go on," Bret commented, "but at least it's something."

They decided to drive to the courthouse to report their progress to Sheriff Buxton. On the way Bret spotted a dark-green pickup truck parked in a side street.

"Bucking broncs!" he exclaimed, braking to a halt. "Look at that, Andy."

A damp wagon sheet covered a bulky load in the back of the truck. In the cab, apparently asleep, lay a man dressed in grimy overalls. A floppy old hat covered the fellow's face.

"Keep an eye on him, Andy," Bret whispered. "I'm going to look under that sheet."

Just as Bret raised it, Andy gave a warning whistle. The cab door opened and the man slid out. He rubbed his eyes sleepily and set the hat on the back of his head.

"Good ol' Texas watermelons, boys," he drawled. "Take your pick. Six bits apiece."

Bret felt foolish as he surveyed the bright-green cargo. He laughed. "Your truck fooled me, mister," he said. "I thought it belonged to somebody else."

"I saw one purty near like this around here last week," the vendor said. "How about a melon, boys?"

Bret pulled out his wallet and bought two.

"Pork chops and watermelons, but no rustlers."

Andy chuckled as they put the melons in their truck. "Now all we need for a picnic is a frying pan and some salt!"

When the boys reached the courthouse, Sheriff Buxton led them into his private office, where he listened to the latest developments.

"I know it looks slow, boys," the sheriff said finally. "But you're making headway. Soon as I get this court session off my hands I'll be in shape to give you more help. Just keep after 'em."

"Thanks, Sheriff," Bret said. "That's what we aim to do."

For the next couple of hours Bret and Andy prowled Tovar's streets and alleys looking for the suspected truck, but with no results. Then, feeling discouraged, they headed back toward the RK.

About four miles out, Bret said quietly, "Up ahead, Andy! A dark-green pickup. I'll pass it so we can get a good look at the driver."

Bret stepped on the gas. He was about to pass the truck when its driver suddenly yanked his hat low over his face and gunned the motor.

"Let's go!" Andy exclaimed, but the advice was not needed. Already Bret had the throttle to the floor.

Swaying wildly on the curves, both vehicles sped side by side. Bret was determined to stop the suspect!

CHAPTER V

A Strange Clue

THE wild, breath-taking chase went on, picking up more and more speed. Then, suddenly, Bret saw his chance. Rounding a short curve on two wheels, the green truck was slow in recovering its balance.

Bret took the curve more skillfully, gunning the pickup to the limit. He was about to wedge the green pickup's left side when a cow suddenly loomed up in the dust-fogged road straight ahead.

The green truck sped safely past the animal, but Bret had no time to swerve. It was either hit the cow or take to the ditch. Bret took to the ditch. He braked sharply. The steering wheel strained like a live thing in his hands. His truck lurched wildly sidewise.

"Wow!" Andy gasped, as the truck lunged to a stop right side up. "Texas was never like this!"

Through the dust Bret could see the green truck speeding away. He knew there would be no chance of overtaking it now.

"Anyhow, I got the license number," Andy said. "It's 13-2586. That's McKinley County, where Ace comes from—Navajo country."

"Let's check the tracks," Bret suggested, climbing out of the cab.

High speed had left the tire marks badly blurred. It took them several minutes to find a clear tire print on the highway's sandy shoulder. Even so, there could be no doubt about it. The tracks matched those they had found on the Rimrock Ranch.

"One more notch on our stick," Andy said. "But what do we do now?"

"All we can do is— Look!" Bret broke off abruptly. "Here comes a car. Let's stop it and ask which road the truck took."

They did not have to wave down the car, a black sedan with a red flasher on the roof. From behind the wheel State Policeman Ed Sanchez saw the truck off the road and stopped to investigate. Briefly, Bret told him what had happened.

"I didn't meet any truck." The black-uniformed trooper shook his head. "Maybe it turned onto a side road. Did you get the license?"

"It was 13-2586," Andy told him.

"Good! I'll radio headquarters to check for the licensee's name."

It took only a moment for him to raise State Police Headquarters in Santa Fe. After a few minutes the reply came through. "Truck license number one-three dash two-five-eight-six," said the voice in Santa Fe, "issued to Alex Begay, a Navajo Indian, at Grants, McKinley County. Begay's truck, a dark-green pickup, was stolen five weeks ago. Has not been recovered."

"It will be," Sanchez spoke into the mike. "Over —and thanks."

"Now while you get back on the road," he told the boys, "I'll alert the State Police on highway patrol, in case this rascal got back onto blacktop. Then we'll go see if we can find which way he went."

This close to town there were numerous side roads. They found that the truck had turned into one of them that led directly to the main highway.

"I guess that's it, boys," Sanchez said. "Once he's on the blacktop we can't track him. But the patrol will surely pick him up. Sorry I can't help you, but I'm on hurry call to Tucumcari to testify in a wreck case."

Bret thanked the trooper, waited while the police car turned around, then started his truck.

"I guess Sanchez is right." Bret sounded discouraged. "We can't trail a truck on the highway. We might as well head for the ranch. Maybe Dad and Benny will have turned up something."

At the ranch Big Jim and Benny had no news for them—except that the lump on Benny's head was just about gone, and that the wire-cut colt was improving.

Bret waited impatiently for a call from the highway patrol. It came around eight that night during a heavy mountain shower.

"State Police office in Tucumcari speaking. Our highway patrol reports no green pickup 13-2586 on highway. Sorry. We'll keep checking."

"Thanks," Bret said, and told his family. "He must have turned off on a cow trail instead of going on to the blacktop. Probably headed for a hide-out somewhere on the range."

"Why don't you boys go there on horseback in the morning?" Big Jim suggested. "That way you can trail this rascal—if he did take to the range."

"Good idea, Dad. I'll phone Vic and see if he and Ace can come along."

"Let Jinx phone ol' Vic and he'll be sure to come." Rusty grinned.

Jinx blushed, but nevertheless telephoned the Eastern boy, who in turn said he would notify Ace.

Vic and Ace drove to the ranch the next morning in time for a hearty breakfast of flapjacks with mountain honey, served by Jinx. While they were eating, Bret and the others saddled seven horses, for this time Jinx and Rusty were going along.

Even by taking short cuts through Rimrock Ranch pastures, Bret figured it would take more than an hour's ride to where he and Andy had lost track of the truck.

The rain of the night before had made the morning crisp and cool. The young folks rode past acres of cane cactus, rosetted with bright cerise blossoms more beautiful than a rose garden. Meadow larks called from the tops of fence posts. A covey of blue quail ran ahead of them, then took wing and whirred away to a rocky hillside.

Ace pointed out an antelope doe with her wobbly young fawn, and moments later a buck with black horns shining in the sun raced them for a little way. Vic and Jinx, riding together, admired the play of colors on rimrock ramparts, changing magically in sun and shadow. But what Bret and Benny admired most was good grass and sleek, fat RK cattle.

"It's a good year," Bret commented as they rode, then added, "if these doggone rustlers don't spoil it."

In high spirits they reached the road where the truck had vanished. But the rain had blurred the tire tracks.

"We'll split up to cover more ground," Bret commanded. "When you find something, yell."

Fifteen minutes later Ace shouted and his companions rode up, full of eager excitement.

"The truck never did go to the blacktop." Ace pointed with his chin, Indian style. "It turned off on this old wood hauler's road. The tracks are very dim—but sure."

"Do you suppose this road leads to a hide-out somewhere on Rimrock property?" Vic asked.

"No telling where a wood road may wind up," Bret replied. "Let's follow these marks and see."

For several miles the truck tracks stayed on the wood road. Then they turned off through a wire gate onto a grassy flat where several big white-faced bulls were grazing.

"This is our bull pasture," Bret explained to Vic. "But don't be nervous. These big fellows are peaceable. Not like— Hey, look!"

A gray airplane with red undermarkings soared suddenly into sight high over Rimrock Mesa. It circled, then swooped low over them and sped away. But the noise of its motor spooked and scattered the bulls.

"Funny business." Bret frowned. One of the bulls had not run, but stood pawing the dirt and rumbling deep in his throat.

"That old surly one is on the fight," Bret said. "We'd better see what ails him."

Riding close, they saw that the bull's nose was whiskered with porcupine quills.

Vic looked astonished. "How in the world do you suppose he got those?"

"Cow critters are curious," Jinx explained, smiling. "Sometimes they stick their noses down to investigate a passing porcupine, and *wham!* The porky's tail slaps their noses full of quills."

"Those truck tracks won't run away," Bret said.

"And that bull's worth five hundred dollars. We'll have to take time to pull those quills or they'll work in and kill him. I'll rope his head. You pick up his heels, Benny, and we'll stretch him out."

The bull shook his head menacingly at the cowboy's approach, but Bret's loop dropped neatly over his horns and yanked tight. The bull sat back on the rope, tossing wildly. Behind him the loop of Benny's catch rope swished down and neatly picked up both hind legs.

With the ropes tied fast to the saddle horns, Bret's and Benny's trained cow horses turned tails to the bull, dug in for a hard pull, and stretched out the animal. Andy jumped off his horse and grabbed the bull's tail to pull him over for a fall. But at that instant Benny's rope broke!

The bull kicked free of its loop, let out a windy snort, and charged at Bret. Taken by surprise, Bret's Kiote failed to side-step quickly enough. The bull's massive head smacked into the horse's shoulder, and down he went, Bret with him.

Jinx cried out in alarm, "Bret, run!"

But Bret was pinned in the saddle. Instead of goring the fallen horse, the bull raced on past, yanking the rope between the struggling horse's hind legs.

"Quick, Andy!" Jinx cried. "Bret'll be killed!"

She rushed in, swinging her loop. The bull whirled to charge at Jinx, but her horse side-stepped in time. The girl's loop yanked tight over the bull's horn's as he lunged past, stopping him momentarily. But the danger was not over.

Bret's horse was up again, with Bret in the saddle. Kiote, now tangled in the rope, kicked and bucked, trying to get his legs free of it.

"Hold on!" Andy called. He leaped from his horse, followed by Rusty. Vic delayed a moment to

untie the slicker from behind his saddle. Then he joined the two others afoot as they ran to aid Bret.

With two quick slashes, Andy's knife cut both ropes. At the same instant, Vic threw his slicker over the bull's head, blinding him, and Rusty grabbed the animal's tail.

The enraged bull tossed the slicker off his horns, whirled, and narrowly missed Rusty. Then suddenly realizing he was loose, he put up his head and charged off.

Bret drew in a long breath and grinned. "Thanks."

"Are you hurt?" Jinx asked.

"Just a few bruises. Come on. Let's get that critter."

After splicing the cut ropes, the boys loped after the bull. Bret and Andy both got ropes on his head, Benny heeled him, Vic and Rusty tailed him over, and they held him down while Jinx pulled out the quills.

It had been a perilous moment, but the riders laughed about it as they continued on, scanning the range for the green truck. Suddenly Rusty, skirting the edge of an arroyo, shouted, "Here it is!"

Wheels in the air, the green truck lay upside down in the gully.

"I hope nobody's underneath it," Jinx said fearfully, as the party rode down into the arroyo. But there was no sign of a driver.

"No doubt he jumped out and headed her over the side," Andy remarked.

Quietly Bret searched for a clue. He found one. Wedged behind the seat cushion was a battered old cowboy hat.

"Our friend must have been in an awful hurry to

leave his bonnet," Bret said as he turned the hat over in his hands. "Hey, look at this!" Clipped to the hatband was the small figure of a Brahma bull, made of black obsidian.

"Bulls and more bulls," Andy joked.

"But this is a curious thing for a hat ornament," commented Bret, pocketing the object. "It may mean something."

Excited over their day's experiences, they rode back to the ranch. There Bret phoned Sheriff Buxton, who promised to salvage the wrecked truck and hold it for possible evidence.

Just at dark that evening Mr. and Mrs. Ortega arrived in a rattly old buckboard. Supper was over, but Jinx and Mrs. King reset the table for them. The Ortegas ate sparingly. It was plain that they were deeply concerned about something. Finally Don Miguel spoke out.

"Señor Jeem," he said, "two strangers want to rent our little *rancho*. Pronto—right away. They offer us so much money! We do not know why."

CHAPTER VI

Signs of a Spy

"WHO are these strangers? What do they want with your ranch?" Big Jim asked.

"They have names not easy for my Spanish tongue," Mr. Ortega replied apologetically. "They are written here on this paper."

Big Jim took the sheet of note paper. Frowning, he read: " 'Dr. Thomas Dudley, Professor William Colfax, Department of Archaeology, Penn's Grove College.' Bone diggers, eh?"

In halting English, Mr. Ortega explained that the strangers wished to excavate and study the old cliff dwellings at the head of Oro Perdido Canyon, and possibly others on the ranch. They proposed to rent the entire place, so they would not be disturbed. Their offer was twelve hundred dollars for the first six months, eighteen for the next.

"That's a lot of money, Don Miguel." Big Jim still looked puzzled. "They must have a grant from one of those rich foundations. Well, money's money, if it comes honestly. I'd advise you to take it—but get a certified check."

"We like to take it," put in Mrs. Ortega, "but the sheep—"

"Why not let them use the old Sabinoso pasture, Jim?" Mrs. King suggested. "It's not much good for cattle, but for sheep it's fine."

"Great idea, Hope."

"We could help them fix up the old house to live in, too," Mrs. King added.

"You are good neighbors, good friends," Mr. Ortega said gravely. "This favor we will accept with gratitude—but only on condition that we pay you some rent."

"Oh, sure," agreed Big Jim, who understood Spanish pride about accepting gratuities. "You can pay me twice what it's worth—and that still won't be much. Have your sheep ready right after noon tomorrow, and we'll help you move. Okay?"

"Hokay—and thank you!" Mr. Ortega nodded to his wife. "But now we must go, Mela. The sky talks of rain, and we must get home to prepare for moving."

Despite the Kings' urgent invitation to stay overnight, the Ortegas took their leave. Half an hour later the thunder-black sky turned loose a drenching, lightning-speared torrent.

"They'll be soaked!" Mrs. King said worriedly. "I wish they had stayed."

"When you live in a dry country," Big Jim observed, "a good soaking can feel good. I wouldn't mind being out in this myself."

He went out on the portal, where Bret and Jinx and Rusty were watching the storm.

"Dad," Bret commented, "two hundred a month is a lot of rent for that Ortega place, just to dig in some old ruins."

"Seems that way to us." Big Jim shrugged. "But then we aren't archaeologists."

Around midnight the rain stopped, and a white-washed moon sailed high over the dripping range.

The next morning Bret was surprised to see Andy and Ace, all mud-spattered, arrive on Andy's motorcycle.

"I have to go to the Box M on an errand," Andy explained. "But Ace has something on his mind."

"Bret," said Ace, as Andy sputtered off down the sloppy road, "all night I've been thinking— why did that airplane make circles over us? Was the pilot looking for somebody else?"

"I've been wondering about that myself," Bret replied. "Why don't we ride out there again for another look?"

Instead of going directly to the scene of the abandoned pickup, the two cowboys rode a wide, ranging, zigzag course. Keen-eyed, they watched both for tracks and any movement that might be a man. But the only marks were those of RK cattle, made since the rain, and the only movement those same cattle.

Then, on a rocky ridgetop a few hundred yards from where the plane had flown over them, Ace suddenly reined up. He pointed.

Instantly Bret saw the clue: two thick-fronded juniper branches lay on the ground a good ten steps from the nearest tree.

"Tree branches don't walk," Ace said significantly. "Somebody broke them off and carried them there."

The Navajo dismounted, picked up the two juniper branches, and held them in front of him. "Somebody hid behind these to watch us down there yesterday."

"Right, Ace! And the plane couldn't land to pick up that somebody because of us and the bulls. Maybe the plane came back later!"

"You speak smart, amigo."

The rain had obliterated the tracks where the spy had lain, but two soggy cigarette butts confirmed their deductions.

From where Bret and Ace stood, the big flat spread out below in plain view. There were no bulls in sight now, but the riders glimpsed the green truck still in the arroyo.

"I guess Sheriff Buxton has other duties besides salvaging stolen trucks," Bret commented. "Likely he'll get around to having it done sometime today. Let's find a way to get down there, Ace."

The boys circled half a mile, picking their way

"Somebody was spying on us yesterday," said Ace

around boulders and slide-rock before they could ride on down to the flat.

Here their own tracks of the day before had been erased by the night's deluge. But they could still see the wallowed-down grass where the bull had bowled over Bret's horse.

"Cowboy in a bullfight leaves much sign," Ace commented tersely. Bret did not miss the twinkle in his friend's black eyes.

"I was just a little too smart for my britches." Bret laughed. "Next time I rope a sore-nosed bull, we won't try to stretch him without two ropes on his head."

"Bad people are worse than bad bulls," observed Ace as he studied the ground. He added, "Looks as if we guessed wrong. No tracks down here."

"We'd better ride out the whole flat," Bret said. "There's plenty of landing room farther on."

Two hundred yards from the scene of the bull ruckus, they found tracks, all but washed out.

"Another bucket of rain and they would have vanished," Bret said wryly.

Ace slid off his horse and studied the marks carefully. By following them painstakingly the boys reached a positive conclusion. These were the tire tracks of a two-wheeled vehicle.

"An airplane, as sure as big ears on a burro," Bret said, and Ace nodded agreement.

They followed the tracks until they disappeared,

evidently at the take-off. But rain had spoiled any chance of verifying their suspicion that the plane had picked up a passenger.

As they turned back, Ace suddenly reined up, raising a hand to his ear in a sign to listen. The hum of a motor seemed to come from two directions.

"A plane!" said Bret.

"A truck!" exclaimed Ace.

Both were right. A plane passed over them, moderately low, and flew on. It looked exactly like the one they had seen the day before, except that there were no red undermarkings. In the glare of the bright sunshine, Bret could not make out the identification numbers.

Hardly was the plane out of sight when a wrecker truck arrived from town with Sheriff Buxton and two men in it.

"We'd have been out sooner," Buxton told Bret, "but I had to help on a roadblock. State Police had a tip on the guys who robbed that bank in Albuquerque awhile back, but they didn't show. You boys have any news?"

Briefly, Bret brought the sheriff up to date on the few baffling clues they had found, and gave him the black obsidian bull trinket. Bret and Ace stayed to help hoist the green pickup out of the arroyo. Together with Sheriff Buxton they combed it over from motor to tail gate, but could find no further clue to the identity of the driver.

When the wrecker was on its muddy way with the truck, Bret and Ace straddled their horses and rode on.

"As long as we're out here," Bret said, "we'd better hunt up that sore-nosed bull and see how he's making out. Sometimes quills go so deep you don't get 'em, and they make trouble."

"Jinx did a good job," Ace said. "If she said all the quills were out, they're all out!"

Bret laughed. In the eyes of his friends Miss Jennifer King could do no wrong, could make no mistake. It amused Bret, but it made him proud of her, too.

They found the bull bedded in a gully with four others. His nose looked swollen, but the way he was peacefully chewing his cud was proof enough that he was recovering.

Bret turned his horse toward one of the several ranch roads fanning out from the Rimrock headquarters.

"We'll help the Ortegas move right after dinner," he told Ace. "We'd better get on back."

They rode awhile in silence, then Ace spoke:

"That little black bull on the hat— When an Indian makes an image," Ace said thoughtfully, "it always means something. But what does this mean?"

Bret was stumped for a reply.

As they turned into the ranch road the riders suddenly came upon Benny, sitting by the roadside. His horse was tied to a nearby tree. Benny grinned at them from under a brand-new hat as he strummed a shiny guitar.

"How come such an expensive hat?" Bret teased him. "Did you rob the Albuquerque bank?"

Grinning mischievously, Benny twanged his guitar and broke into song:

> *"Git along little dogie,*
> *Good luck for little Benny!*
> *He'll fly in the clouds,*
> *And it won't cost a penny!"*

"Right pretty tune," Bret commented. "But what the dickens do you mean by it?"

Benny tilted his new sombrero at a rakish angle, mounted, and strummed a few more chords before answering.

"These fellows Colfax and Dudley who rent our ranch," he explained finally, "they came in *un aeroplano*. They promised to take me for some rides. All I got to do is keep everybody away from Oro Perdido Canyon."

CHAPTER VII

Chopo in Trouble

THE faces of Bret and Ace showed amazement. "Did they explain why?" Bret asked.

"Sure," Benny replied. "Some other archaeo—what-you-may-call-its—also want to discover some prehistorics in the cliff dwellings. But if these ones discover first, it makes them a big honor. So they want to keep everything a secret."

"You know," said Bret thoughtfully, "that's the same sort of talk they put out about Los Alamos where they developed the atomic bomb. Do you suppose this could be another secret government project?"

"Quién sabe?" Benny said. "Whatever they do is okay with me, just so I get a ride in their airplane."

Bret did not pursue the subject further. Instead, he snatched Benny's new hat and looked inside at the label.

"Four X Bever!" he exclaimed. "You'll never

get rich buying twenty-five-dollar hats! And that guitar must have cost even more."

"If I am a fine cowboy, I have to wear a fine hat," Benny explained happily, accurately describing a custom of the cow country. "But it comes not from wages. Those fellows paid for the ranch in cash. Right away Papa gave me money to spend how I like."

Ace frowned. "Most folks these days pay such amounts by check."

"Maybe they pay cash because it is a government secret. Anyhow, how do you like my new sombrero?"

"It's a dillywhacker all right." Bret handed it back to him. "But it will look more like a cowboy's hat after a few cows have stepped on it."

Benny laughed. "This afternoon we Ortegas move to the Sabinoso. If you help, maybe some time I'll let you wear my fine hat."

"We've already promised Don Miguel to help," Bret assured him. "We'll go by the ranch and get the pickup to haul the furniture and stuff."

At the ranch, however, the boys found the truck gone and nobody at home. This made Bret feel uneasy for a moment, until he found a note Big Jim had stuck on the corral gate. It wasted no words:

"Bret: We've gone. Come on."

Stopping only for a glass of milk, some cold biscuits, and honey, Bret, Benny, and Ace hurried on to the Ortega place in Oro Perdido Canyon.

By the time the boys arrived, Big Jim and Rusty were helping the Ortegas load their household goods. Jinx and her mother were nowhere in sight. When Bret asked about them, his father winked and shook his head.

"Maybe gone fishin'." Big Jim shook his head again, which Bret took to mean "don't ask."

When the loading was finished, the rancher drove the pickup. Mrs. Ortega rode with him. The rest followed more slowly on horseback, driving the sheep and goats before them.

Looking back over the meadow, Bret had a good view of the cliff dwellings farther up the canyon. As a young boy he had been up there once. But Bret's main interest was in live horses and cattle rather than in dead ruins. Now, however, his curiosity had been aroused by the events of the past few days.

"Benny," he said, "what makes you afraid of those cliff-dweller ruins?"

"*Chisos*—ghosts!"

Bret was surprised at Benny's earnestness.

"A long time ago another boy and I went to explore those ruins. We found many caves dug into the cliffs. But we did not stay long."

"A ghost in every room, I suppose," Bret teased him. "How many did you see?"

"None," Benny replied, looking sober. "But we heard one. It sounded something like this—"

Benny made a round mouth. The noise he produced was a weird quavering, halfway between a soft, sirenlike whistle and a moan.

"Then it made like a scream," he added. "We come away quick."

"It might have been the wind," Bret suggested, as Don Miguel rode up alongside him.

"No, no, *hijo!*" Don Miguel contradicted him. "It is the ghost of a soldier. My grandfather told me. This Spaniard came looking for gold hidden by Indians. But a brave grabbed the soldier's sword and split his head with it."

Rusty's eyes widened and he gulped. "Gee, did the Indians really have gold hidden up there, Don Miguel?"

"My grandfather believed it—and in the ghost, too."

"Weren't you afraid to live so close to a spook?" Rusty went on.

"No, hijo." Don Miguel's wrinkles spread in a smile. "My grandfather make bargain with ghost for all Ortegas: if we don't bother ghost, he don't bother us!"

"It's an interesting legend," Bret commented. To himself he said, "Perhaps Colfax and Dudley are looking for that gold!"

Ace, who had been silent all through the discussion, now spoke quietly.

"In the country of the Navajo there are places that belong to the ghost people. There my people do not go. I suppose we cannot blame Benny for running away."

Bret had learned to respect the Indian's belief in supernatural things, and remained discreetly silent. He fixed his attention on the livestock. The goats, commonly used to lead sheep, had been trotting out ahead in the right direction and all was well.

Now all of a sudden a whiskery old billy goat quit the herd, circled back around a rocky hillside, and struck out for Oro Perdido Canyon.

"Goat roping's about the right size for you and that midget mustang," Bret called to Rusty. "Go get him!"

"Yippee!" Rusty whooped. "Come on, Chopo!" The pinto Shetland sped after the billy goat, with Rusty letting out his rope. Ace followed close enough to give help if needed.

The goat stuck to the rocky hillside. Rusty put Chopo up the slope, and swinging his rope in real cowboy style, the young boy dabbed the loop neatly over the billy's horns. At the same instant, Chopo, sure-footed though he was, skidded on a loose rock and went down on his knees.

Rusty stayed aboard. But when the goat felt the rope yank on his head, he turned and raced back. Stretching the lariat tight, the animal started running circles around Rusty and his horse, winding the rope around the pony's legs.

Bret saw the danger and took off at a dead run

to help. But Ace was there ahead of him. The Indian leaned low from the saddle and yanked Rusty's rope off the goat's horns. With the rope loosened, Rusty quickly freed his feet from the stirrups, stepped off the pony, pulled in the slack, and had Chopo's legs untangled by the time Bret got there.

The goat, meanwhile, had started off again at a run, this time down on the flat. At a smooth, fast

gallop Ace overtook the animal. He bent down, seized a horn, and dragged the astonished billy back to the herd.

"Well, gee my wheeze!" Benny exclaimed as they all started on. "Which is the worst, a ghost or a goat?"

Rusty looked crestfallen, blaming himself for

the accident. But he cheered up when Bret gave him a brotherly whack on the shoulder and said with a grin, "You did all right, kid. I've seen top-hand cowpokes in the same kind of a fix."

After that, neither goats nor sheep gave any more trouble. As they came in sight of the little adobe house that was to be the Ortegas' temporary home, Benny spied two saddled horses hitched in the shade of a cottonwood.

"Look! Somebody's there!" he exclaimed. "Rustlers maybe!"

This idea was quickly dispelled when Jinx and Mrs. King appeared in the doorway.

"Welcome to your new home!" Jinx called out. She and her mother had ridden over early to clean up the place. Big Jim had arrived with the furniture and helped Mrs. Ortega set it up while the two Rimrock women had cooked supper for the new tenants.

"Good neighbors," Don Miguel said simply, "are the gift of God."

It was getting late, so the Kings stayed only long enough to have coffee with the Ortegas. Then they started back to the ranch. Mrs. King went with her husband in the pickup, but Jinx rode back with the boys, trailing her mother's horse.

Rounding a sharp peninsula of the mesa just at sunset, they suddenly came upon two big bulls in terrific battle.

"Good bulls can get badly hurt in a fight," said Bret. "I'd better see if I can break it up. The rest of you watch out. Whenever a bull decides he's whipped, he'll run like a locomotive—right over anything in his way."

Quickly Jinx rode up protectively between Rusty and the bulls. All of a sudden one of the animals bellowed, whirled, and took off like a shot—straight toward Jinx!

CHAPTER VIII

Unfriendly Neighbors

ALONE, Jinx might have had time to whirl her horse out of the way. But her first thought was of Rusty. The instant the bull broke away, she leaned over and quirted Chopo hard across the rump.

"Quick, Rusty!" she cried out. "Yank him to the right!"

Rusty obeyed. But when the girl tried to turn her horse the same way, Silky bumped into the Shetland. The vanquished bull, closely followed by the victor, came rushing headlong toward Jinx, blind to everything except his own desperate urge to escape.

Both Ace and Bret saw the danger and spurred their horses after the bulls at a breakneck run. For a tense moment it was a race with death.

Bret's Kiote was a quarter horse, always fast on the getaway, and faster still under the desperate prod of spurs. The fleeing bull was within a dozen yards of Jinx when Bret overtook him.

The cowboy leaned from the saddle and grabbed the fear-maddened animal's tail. He jerked it up to a quick wrap around his saddle horn. At the same time, he turned his horse sharply to the right. For one brief second he was able to keep his grip on the lunging animal's tail. Then he felt it slip and jerk loose.

But that one second had been enough to pull the panicked bull off his course. Still bent on getting far away quickly, the big old surly kept right on going—in the changed direction. He thundered past Jinx and Rusty, missing them by a safe twenty feet.

Ace, coming on behind, slapped his rope across the pursuing bull's eyes, turning him as well.

Rusty looked up at his tall brother with wide-eyed admiration. "Gee, Bret, he'd have run over us for sure if you hadn't tailed him!"

"Maybe not," Bret said gravely. "But it was a close thing. My fault for breaking up the fight."

"It *wasn't* your fault," Jinx protested warmly. "He started to run before you ever got near them."

"She's right, Bret." Ace nodded.

All of them felt shaken by the narrow escape and as they rode on to the ranch there was little conversation.

Big Jim and Mrs. King had arrived, and Vic Martinson was there from town.

"Father let me off for tomorrow," Vic told Bret. "If I can be of assistance—"

"You sure can," Bret broke in. "Don Miguel tells me Colfax and Dudley are coming tomorrow morning. We'll offer to help them—and keep our eyes open."

"Okay, Bret." Vic turned to Jinx. "I'll unsaddle and rub down Silky for you," he offered.

"Love me, love my horse!" Rusty chortled.

If Jinx took his teasing seriously, she did not show it. More or less as a matter of habit, she yanked out Rusty's shirttail, then turned to Vic with a friendly smile.

"I'm glad you came, Vic," she said. "From what I hear, you may be able to help."

The next morning Benny was already waiting at the Ortega place when Bret, Ace, Vic, and Rusty reined up in Oro Perdido Canyon. Shortly afterward, a two-ton truck, loaded with heavy-looking boxes, lumbered in. At the wheel was a tall, thin man who had an exaggerated Adam's apple and squinty eyes. Bret judged the driver to be in his early thirties. Beside him in the cab sat two husky men. The thin man stepped out, frowning, and addressed the riders.

"I'm Professor William Colfax. What are you boys doing here?"

"We're your neighbors from the Rimrock Ranch," Bret answered politely. "Thought you might like help moving in."

"I've got Jones and Wiley here," Colfax said. "We don't need anyone else."

"We could help carry those big boxes," Rusty offered. "They sure look heavy. What's in 'em— machinery?"

"If it's any of your business, which it isn't," Colfax replied coldly, keeping his narrow-set eyes on Bret, "it's special equipment for the secret scientific work we expect to be carrying on here."

"Gee my wheeze!" Benny exclaimed. "We heard you were bone diggers."

"You heard right," Colfax said bluntly. "We're archaeologists. Now beat it!"

"Looks as if we wore out our welcome mighty fast," Bret drawled. "Well, let's—"

He broke off abruptly as a small gray airplane swooped in low from the direction of the mesa. For a minute the boys had their hands full with the rearing and plunging of their spooked horses. By the time they got them quieted, the plane had landed on the flat.

Bret was sure he had seen two men in the cockpit, but only one got out. Carrying a suitcase in one hand, a brief case in the other, the fellow strode briskly to the house where the truckers were preparing to unload. He was a short, stocky man. His square face wore a wide smile.

"Good morning, Professor Colfax," he said. Then he turned to the boys. "Neighbors?" One blond eyebrow lifted inquiringly. "I'm Professor Colfax's colleague, Dr. Dudley."

Briefly, Bret made introductions and renewed the offer to help.

"Why, certainly. Thank you." Dudley sounded good-natured and friendly. "Glad to have you."

All five stepped from their horses and went to work. Even Dudley took a brisk hand at the unloading.

"You fellows seem to be cowboys," he commented. "Do you live near here?"

"That depends on whether you're afoot, on horseback, in a car, or in an airplane," Bret replied a little warily. "How are things in Wyoming?"

"Wyoming?" Dudley's jovial expression vanished. "You mean Wyoming County, Pennsylvania, of course."

"I didn't know there was one by that name in the East," Bret replied, smiling. He pointed to the shiny Wyoming license plate on the truck. "That's the one I mean."

Dudley eased a box to the ground and stood ramrod straight. "The scientific work we're preparing to carry on here—for Penn's Grove College—is strictly top secret. You would be wise to curb your curiosity. As for that truck, we hired it to bring in some equipment."

"You say it mighty plain." Bret shrugged. "Is this big box next?"

"Right. Lend a hand here."

As they jockeyed the heavy packing case out of the truck, Dudley's hold on one corner of it slipped. Bret jerked his foot out of the way just in time to keep it from being crushed.

"Sorry," Dudley said. But his voice sounded so curt that Bret wondered whether the box had been allowed to drop on purpose. And why, he thought, had the reference to Wyoming rattled the new-comer?

"Caution's the word, cowboy," Bret told himself

in a silent warning. "You can't catch coyotes by whooping and hollering at their tracks."

The silence was broken by Rusty, who had been staring off toward the parked airplane.

"Hey, Mr. Dudley," he asked, "how come the other man stays in the plane? Is he sleeping or something?"

"Oh, you mean the pilot?" Dudley replied, again seeming good-humored. "He just happens to be one of those high-chinned fellows who considers himself above anything but flying a plane."

"I've never seen the inside of an airplane," Rusty said. "May I take a look?" He stepped forward a few paces.

"Hold on, you little squirt!" exclaimed Colfax sharply. He seized Rusty by the arm and jerked him back.

Bret got to them in three long strides. He grabbed Colfax by the collar of his shirt and whirled him around.

"Easy on the rough stuff, Colfax," he said quietly. "Rusty's just a kid."

Scowling, Colfax stepped back, doubling his fists.

"Cut it out, Col!" Dudley said fiercely. "We don't want no trouble with these boys." Muttering under his breath, Colfax turned and went into the house.

"Now, friends," Dudley said with a forced smile, "you've been a big help to us, and I thank you. But

I've made it plain that from now on visitors will not be welcome here. Good-by!"

Bret felt a surge of anger at the blunt dismissal. Dudley had a right to order them off, but they would not hurry. Quietly the boys went to their horses, reset their saddles, and adjusted the cinches.

Wiley frowned impatiently. Suddenly he blurted out, "Listen, you punks! You've been told. Get going, and from now on, if you know what's good for you, *stay out of Oro Perdido Canyon!*"

Benny looked startled. "You mean me, too?"

"Especially you," Wiley snapped. "You Mexican chili picker!"

His eyes ablaze, Benny leaped at Wiley like a banty fighting cock.

CHAPTER IX

Trick Riding

BENNY'S right fist thumped Wiley solidly in the middle. His left skidded off the bully's chin. But before either combatant could strike another blow, Bret and Ace got between them. Even Dudley took a hand, seizing Wiley's arms to hold him back.

"That'll do, Wiley!" Dudley spoke in a tone of authority. "What if the kid is a Mexican?"

"Now look here!" Vic addressed Dudley and his companions in a quiet voice that did not conceal his indignation. "Let's cut out the name calling! Benny Ortega's people were pioneers here even before the *Mayflower* landed. This land has been theirs for centuries, handed down from a royal Spanish grant."

"You tell 'em, Vic!" Bret could not wait to express his approval.

"The Ortegas," Vic went on, "became citizens

of the United States when General Kearny raised the Stars and Stripes over New Mexico in 1846. And they've been loyal Americans ever since."

The intensity of the boy's rebuke brought beads of perspiration to his face, and a look of respect to Dudley's.

"Hold on!" Dudley spoke soothingly. "No need to get steamed up over a little slip of the tongue. I'm sure Benny's okay. We apologize, don't we, Wiley?"

The man muttered something, then said aloud, "Okay, Doc, I spoke out of turn."

"All right, boys," said Bret between tight drawn lips. "That settles it. Now let's go."

As they rode away, Ace turned in the saddle, swung his hat in a circle over his head, and let out a wild yell that sounded like a defiant coyote. Coming from the usually quiet Navajo, the outburst surprised the other boys.

"Say, you really can holler!" Rusty exclaimed. "What was that for?"

"Navajo war medicine." Ace spoke with mock soberness, a twinkle in his black eyes. "Heap big scarum talk, you savvy?"

"I savvy Vic sure got those buzzards told," Benny said earnestly. "I'm much obliged to you, Vic."

"I would have enjoyed seeing you administer a first-rate punching to the Wiley fellow," Vic replied.

Bret shook his head. "It wouldn't have helped us solve this truck rustling problem. And that's our main job right now."

They rode on silently for a while until Vic spoke. "Bret, don't you think this would be a good time to re-evaluate our suspicions and the evidence?"

"If you mean now's a good time to tally clues," Bret replied with a grin, "you're dead right. Where shall we start?"

"Well, to begin with," Vic said, "we know that Rimrock steers have been butchered by thieves. One was shot with a gun used for the same purpose in Wyoming. That means the truck rustling is more than a local operation."

"Next," Bret carried on, "we're reasonably sure none of the stolen beef was sold in Tovar, and that it was hauled off the ranch by the same pickup truck we found abandoned in the arroyo. Also, the truck was driven by a man wearing a little obsidian Brahma bull on an old flop hat."

"Probably the whiskered man whom Otto Mueller described to you and Andy," Vic continued. "And we're pretty sure a plane picked him up."

"But what about those shoe tracks where the steer hide was buried?" Benny asked.

"Not so good," said Ace. "The rain erased the tracks of the man who left the truck. Today I tried to see the shoe prints of all four men at the Ortega place. The ground was too hard to take a good print. But I think none was the same as the tracks near the steer hide."

Rusty spoke up. "There were red markings on the plane that spied on us near the wrecked truck, but this one today was plain gray."

"Painted, maybe," Ace suggested.

"Quite possible," said Vic. "However, I got this plane's identification number."

"How about the pilot remaining inside the plane?" Bret asked. "Something mysterious there."

"Maybe he was afraid the ghost of the cliff dwellings would get him," Rusty offered.

Bret chuckled, but grew serious again. "I can't help feeling suspicious of this whole outfit. Did you notice that *Doctor* Dudley said 'we don't want no trouble'? Wouldn't a Ph.D. use more correct grammar, Vic?"

"Absolutely."

"Well, gee my wheeze! If Papa had some suspicion of crooks, he never would have rent them the place!"

"We know that," Bret assured Benny.

"Anyhow, Benny got a new hat and guitar out of it," Rusty said teasingly. He reached over to tickle Benny's horse in the flank. The horse promptly kicked up his heels. But the cowboy enjoyed the little wingding. He twanged an imaginary guitar and burst into song:

"O Mama, O Papa, be good to your son,
For he is a rough ridin' son of a gun!
But what worries Benny and gives him a pain:
He won't get to ride in an air-ee-o-plane!"

"Maybe you will at that," Bret said. "Well, we've got *some* evidence and a lot of suspicions, but no deadwood on anybody—yet."

Their discussion had made the ride to the ranch pass quickly. Half a mile from the house they met Jinx on her pet palomino, Silky. She was out on a smooth flat, practicing trick riding, but quit and rode on with them.

When they told her of the morning's events, Jinx came up with an idea of her own. "I'll write to Penn's Grove College," she said, "and find out whether they're really sponsoring this Dudley-Colfax project."

"Good girl," Bret said approvingly.

"And I'll check on that plane's identification number," Vic added.

"If the rest of you will tend to the horses," Bret suggested, "Vic and I will go in the house and talk this over with Dad."

Instead of taking the horses to the corral immediately, the other four turned back to the nearby flat for a little horseback frolic. Ace tried to show Jinx and Rusty how to swing themselves under a horse's neck from one side to the other with the horse at full gallop.

Jinx knew that this maneuver was one of the hardest stunts in any trick rider's repertoire, but Ace accomplished it smoothly on Silky.

"Now you try," Ace said to Jinx after a couple of runs.

Because the trick cannot be done safely with an ordinary stock saddle, Jinx had equipped her saddle with the necessary "catch straps"—strong leather thongs hanging down a foot or so at the front of the saddle on each side—to be used for handholds.

Slim and graceful, Jinx mounted her horse. She put Silky into a long, smooth gallop, then swung out of the saddle on his left side and began the underneck crawl. On the first run she did not quite make it. But she did manage to tug herself back up into the saddle without taking a fall—not an easy stunt in itself.

"Keep your legs doubled up close to the horse," Ace advised her. "All weight of the body must be supported by one hand while the other reaches for the catch strap on the other side. Remember, never let go one hand unless the other has a sure hold."

On the third run Jinx made it, and even Ace waved his hat and cheered.

"Now watch me do it," Rusty boasted, putting Chopo into a gallop. He had himself halfway under the pony's neck, when Chopo swerved to one side, directly over a clump of cactus. Rusty's pants seat was swinging too low.

"Ow!" Rusty yelled, and fell, rolling. But he got up unhurt—except for a few cactus spines. As he gingerly removed them, Ace looked on without the trace of a smile.

"Good show, Rusty. Do it again!"

"Quit kidding me, Ace. Ow! I can't get this one out. How about a hand?"

The Navajo assisted until all the spines were removed. Then the horses were corralled.

Jinx was first into the house. She found Bret, Vic, and Big Jim holding a serious council. Bret was suggesting that they ask Sheriff Buxton to post a lookout on the road that led into the Ortega place.

"With truck rustling going on in Wyoming, Colorado, and all around," Bret argued, "it could be all one big operation. If so, there's more than four or five involved in it—and we've got to find out who they are."

"You're right, son," Big Jim said soberly. "We'll phone Buxton right now."

Before Bret could get to the phone, it rang. Buxton himself was calling.

"New developments." The sheriff sounded urgent. "I want Big Jim and you boys to meet me right away. Come to my home as soon as you can —it's more private there than the office—and we've got to be careful!"

CHAPTER X

Counterspies

"ALL right, son, let's go!" Big Jim reached for his hat. "We'll take Ace and Vic. Jinx, you get Rusty to help with the chores. Benny had better ride the west steer pasture till dark."

"Jim"—Mrs. King laid a hand on his arm as he strode out—"I know it's never any use to ask a cowman when he'll be back, but you and the boys be careful, will you?"

"Why, sure, honey!" Big Jim spoke gently. "You don't think I'd risk leaving a pretty woman like you a widow, do you?"

Bret could see that the smile which passed between them was one of complete understanding, and it warmed his heart.

Bret really hit the high spots driving to town, and for once Big Jim did not caution him to slow down.

There was nothing fancy about Buxton's somewhat weathered, vine-covered cottage on the outskirts of Tovar. Some folks said the fact that his family lived in such a modest home was pretty fair proof he was an honest sheriff.

Andy and his father hurried out to greet the Rimrock Ranch party as they arrived.

"Glad you could come!" The sheriff wasted no words on greetings. "Let's go into my den. It's more private."

This was the first time Vic and Ace had seen Buxton's collection of frontier firearms. Their eyes literally bugged at the racks of everything from long-barreled Sharps buffalo rifles to a snub-nosed little derringer.

"Just a hobby, boys," Buxton told them. "I'd be glad if I could hang up this six-shooter with the rest of them. But as long as there's outlawing— Well, find seats and I'll tell you what's itching me."

Sheriff Buxton lighted his pipe. "Now here's the skunk cabbage," he said, "and it smells plenty bad. Truck rustlers have hit the Flying Spur—fifteen head of fat steers in a week. Only two hides found. Bill Evans—you know the Flying Spur manager, Big Jim—figures the rest may have been hauled off alive."

Big Jim shook his head doubtfully. "Those Spur cattle are pretty wild for truck loading on the range without a chute, Sheriff."

Instead of answering, Buxton handed Bret a stockmen's journal folded open at a marked paragraph, which Bret read aloud:

" 'It is reported that Montana truck rustlers dope steers they intend to steal by shooting into them a pellet of powerful tranquilizer from a noise- less gun. The critter is thus rendered docile enough to load easily into a truck. . . .' "

"Well, I'll be a burro's uncle!" Bret exclaimed.

"Of course we know some outfits use tranquil- izer hypodermics on their own cattle to prevent un- due excitement in shipping," said Big Jim, "but I never heard of thieves using it this way."

"We've got no proof of any such doings on the Flying Spur," Buxton went on. "But from the way the rustlers seem to know right where to pick up cattle without getting caught, I've got a mighty strong hunch they've got a spotter spying for them on the inside."

"You mean one of the Spur's own cowboys may be in league with the rustlers?" Vic asked.

"That's right—one or more. The Flying Spur is a walloping big ranch," Buxton explained. "Runs a lot of different kinds of stock. Bill Evans has to suit the big owners back East. They natu- rally don't keep a full crew through the slack seasons. So Bill has to hire drifters—most any kind of a cowboy that comes along—for times when the cow work's heavy."

"Which makes a good opening for thieves and outlaws," Andy added. "Right now, Evans has a big work in progress. He's branding, vaccinating, and dehorning a herd of Chihuahua steers imported from Mexico. So he's been hiring drifters for some time."

"That's where you and Ace come in, Bret," said the sheriff. "Will you boys hire out to the Flying Spur as drifters, under assumed names of course, and do a little sleuthing? Maybe you can pick up information that'll help us get the deadwood on these truck rustlers."

"Will a fish swim, Mr. Sheriff?" asked Ace, an eager gleam in his eyes.

"I've already picked my alias, Sheriff!" Bret spoke excitedly. "Meet Rawhide Ray Johnson, just a wandering waddy from Wampus, Arizona! When do we start?"

"Monday morning will be soon enough," Buxton replied. "You got an alias picked, too, Ace?"

"How do you like 'Jake Martinez'?"

"Fine! I've fixed it with Bill to hire you on as strangers. Now I don't want you to risk getting yourselves shot or anything like that. Just keep your eyes and ears open, and here—take this," the sheriff added, handing Bret the little bull figure. "It may lead you to the man who's spying on the Spur."

"Excuse me, Mr. Sheriff." Ace suddenly looked worried. "Maybe this won't work so well after all. The horse wrangler on the Spur, Pete Kyler, is a good friend of ours. He'll recognize us both."

"That's right. I know Ky," said Bret.

Sheriff Buxton's frown cleared as quickly as it

appeared. "But I'll fix that. I'm to meet Evans in Las Vegas tomorrow. I'll get him to tip off Ky— and anybody else on the crew he thinks might recognize you—not to let on they know you."

Buxton turned to Big Jim, who had sat silent through most of the discussion.

"I reckon I ought to have asked your approval of this plan first, Jim. Of course if you say it's no go—"

"You know me better than that, Buck," Big Jim said. "These boys can take care of themselves. Meantime, if you'll spare Andy, I'll mount him and Vic to ride the Rimrock in the Oro Perdido country and keep an eye on the comings and goings of Dudley and Colfax. Benny and Jinx and Rusty and me—we'll ride the beef pastures. That ought to—"

"Dad! Sheriff! Look!" Bret exclaimed sharply. "There at the window!"

"Where?" asked Buxton. "I don't see anything."

"I saw a man's hat a second ago!" Bret said. "If it was somebody spying—listening in on our plans—"

Without finishing the sentence, Bret dashed outside, quickly followed by Ace and Andy. They saw a battered car parked a hundred yards down the road, but nobody in it. As Bret started to search around the cottage, a short man in wrinkled slacks and sport shirt turned the corner of the dwelling.

"Hi there," he greeted Bret. "Knocked but nobody answered. I need to borrow a lug wrench. Just my luck—a flat tire and no wrench."

The stranger pointed toward the car down the road. Bret checked an impulse to ask the man if he thought peeking in a window was a good way to find a lug wrench. But after all, he thought, the fellow looked and sounded innocent enough.

Bret got a wrench from their truck, and the boys helped the motorist change his tire.

"I wonder about this guy," Andy said, after the man had driven off. "Why didn't he walk to the gas station down the street?"

"I have good ears," Ace said. "I never heard him knock."

"Colorado plates," said Vic. "We should have gotten the license number, but since we really have nothing on him, I don't suppose it matters."

"The idea of his eavesdropping on us worries me," said Bret.

Still uncertain whether they had missed a bet by not detaining the man for questioning, the sleuthing party broke up. Big Jim and Bret drove back to the ranch. Vic, Andy, and Ace stayed in town, promising to drive out in Vic's jalopy the next evening, ready to continue the hunt for the rustlers Monday morning.

The three boys arrived at the ranch early enough to share a Sunday supper of cold fried chicken, potato salad, milk, coffee, and one of Jinx's cakes.

Later, the family gathered on the porch, listening to the gentle whir of the crickets' song. For a while Benny strummed his guitar, then Mrs. King started a hymn in which everybody joined.

It was difficult at this moment for the Rimrock folks to believe that sinister outlaws menaced their peace.

Bret retired early and got a good night's sleep. An hour before dawn he and Ace had piled their saddles and bedrolls in the rattly jalopy Vic had loaned them and were ready to roll.

"Arizona plates!" Ace commented.

"Buxton's taking no chances," Bret replied.

Mrs. King made no fuss about the boys' going. She had been a ranch wife too long to question anything her menfolks felt obliged to do.

"Good luck," she told them, "and don't step off any rimrocks with your eyes shut!"

Big Jim gave each a firm handshake.

As the jalopy covered the hilly miles in the rosy rays of sunrise, the boys fell to reviewing again the past week's exciting events.

"One thing," Ace said. "I forgot to ask Big Jim to look at the tire tracks of the lug-wrench man. He might be the same rock hunter who knocked down the gate where your colt was cut."

"Just so we don't forget our new names, Señor Jake Martinez!"

"Okay, Roy Johnson! No more 'Ace' and 'Bret' for now."

Just as the sun came up, they reached the Flying Spur headquarters. Its buildings and corrals sprawled out farther and were somewhat less neatly kept than those at the Rimrock Ranch. But they looked and smelled "cow ranch."

The lizardlike hills and rock-rimmed mesas that surrounded the place sheltered a vast assortment of grassy draws and valleys. Eastward beyond all these, the vista widened into open plains, still Flying Spur range as far as the eye could see.

Bill Evans, a medium-built, middle-aged man, with the look of a cow hand from hat to boot heel, rode up from the corrals to meet them as soon as he heard the jalopy arrive. Even with no one else around, he gave no sign that Bret and Ace were anything but drifter-strangers.

In less than two minutes and twice two dozen words, he hired them.

"Throw your stuff in the bunkhouse, boys," he told them, "and step on it. We're saddling up."

Saddles on their shoulders, Bret and Ace hurried to the corrals. There the leathery Spur range boss, Dwight Jenkins, was roping the day's mounts out of the remuda as each cowboy called the name of the horse he wanted.

Bill Evans introduced "Roy Johnson" and "Jake Martinez" to him briefly.

"Give 'em ol' Daybreak and Shogood for today, Jenkins," he ordered. "We'll pick out full strings for them later."

Halfway around the corral Bret saw something that made him shudder. A tall, whiskery cowboy was walloping his horse over the head with his rope. Neither Evans nor Jenkins saw it, but the slim young wrangler, Pete Kyler, did. He stepped up and grabbed the big cow hand's rope before he could swing it again.

"Easy on the rough stuff, Williams," Ky said. "We don't abuse horses around here!"

With no word of warning, Williams swung his fist. It connected. Ky went sprawling in the dust.

"Mind your own business, punk!" Williams snarled, and raised his right leg to kick the boy.

Bret got there fast. He yanked Williams around angrily and slammed a left jab to his jaw!

CHAPTER XI

Rough and Tumble

WILLIAMS teetered on his boot heels but quickly regained his balance and lunged at Bret, head down like an angry bull. The boy had been all set for defense against fists, but not this wild, lunging attack. His own fist grazed the side of Williams' head, but did not stop the big man.

Grappling, the two rolled over and over. Bret preferred a stand-up battle, but if it had to be rough and tumble, he was ready.

Bret's right arm squirmed free. With catlike speed it clamped a near hammer lock around his adversary's neck. Straining every muscle, Bret arched himself against the heavier man's weight and heaved the bully over on his back. This brought Bret out on top, momentarily straddling a writhing bundle of muscular dynamite. Bret cocked his fist to drive at the contorted form beneath him when the iron grip of Bill Evans' hand seized his arm. At the same instant, Bill's boot pinned one of Williams' hairy wrists to the ground.

"Break it up, you two!" The Spur manager's voice was cold with anger. "Here, Jenkins, help me unscramble these yahoos!"

But the foreman did not have to help. At the voice of authority, Bret jerked free, rolled over, and came up on his feet. Williams rose slowly, staring at the little black Brahma amulet that had fallen from Bret's pocket in the ruckus.

Before Williams could stoop to pick it up, Ace's brown hand seized it. He slipped the object quickly into his pocket and strode off to where Jenkins was again swinging his loop for the next horse.

"Now hark and heed, you two!" Bill Evans' voice had the hard, sharp edge of a chisel. "We're running a cow-work here, not prize fights. Any more of this monkey business and I'll fire you both! Savvy?"

"Yes, sir," said Bret, but Williams only scowled and said nothing. This was Bret's chance for a good look at his enemy's face. It was hard and bristly, with black stubble and bushy eyebrows. Bret felt a quiver of excitement cavort up and down his spine as he noted that the man's mouth was like a wide, ugly gash across his face, almost from ear to ear. This could be the man who tried to sell the beef to Otto Mueller.

As Williams turned away, one of the other cowboys called out to him. "Hey, Wide Mouth! Come get your horse!"

A hand touched Bret's arm. It was Pete Kyler. "Much obliged, *stranger*," he said. "He had me in a bad fix."

Bret was glad no one but Evans was near enough to see Ky's broad wink.

"Think nothing of it, kid," Bret said. "I never did like a horse walloper, anyhow."

As Kyler walked away, Evans approached. He spoke in a low tone to Bret. "Play it quiet, Bret. Blowing your lid won't get us anywhere."

Bret nodded and went to saddle up the blaze-faced bay called Daybreak that Jenkins roped out for him. Ace was already lacing his hull on a lively black called Shogood.

"Well, gee my wheeze!" Ace said softly, imitating Benny Ortega's grin. "Mr. Rawhide Roy Johnson plays rough, *qué no?*"

"Sometime I'll choose me the wrong rooster, Jake," Bret said smilingly, "and lose my feathers."

Earning their wages as cow hands the rest of that day left Bret and Ace no chance to talk privately. The work was all riding, gathering cattle. Daybreak and Shogood proved to be first-class mounts, and the boys thoroughly enjoyed riding them.

Evans had shipped in a big herd of Chihuahuas

three weeks before. Bought cheaply on drought-stricken range, the Mexican cattle had arrived too poor and gaunt to stand immediate branding and dehorning. So Bill Evans had turned them out to get some grass in their bellies and strength in their bodies before working them.

Unlike the well-bred Herefords on the Rimrock Ranch and on other parts of the Flying Spur, the Chihuahuas were of no uniform color, shape, or size. Speckles, line-backs, reds, duns, roans, browns, grays, even a few whites—they were exactly what Bret called them, "crazy-quilt cattle."

Long of horn, ridge-backed and shanky, in their present shape they would offer no temptation to beef thieves. But Evans had been shrewd in buying such low-grade cattle. They would fatten on the Spur's rich grass, and every pound they put on would be clear profit.

In one respect they were all alike—as wild as deer and almost as hard to drive. Hazing them out of rocky canyons and scrub-oak thickets, and across cactus-brambled flats into the holding pasture called for hard and skillful riding.

To Bret and Ace it was exciting adventure. Yet they could not throw off the uneasy feeling that they were getting nowhere in their search for the truck rustlers.

At headquarters that evening, between unsaddling at the corrals and the supper gong, they had a chance to speak briefly to Evans alone.

Williams, Evans told them, had been signed on two weeks before. Evans had let him bunk at the ranch, but with cow work slack, had not actually put him on the pay roll until a few days ago.

"That fits," Bret said. "I think Wide Mouth is our man. But we'll need proof. To nab him on suspicion won't help much. We want to trap the whole big truck rustler organization."

"Right," Evans agreed. Then he raised his voice as Williams and another cowboy passed within hearing. "All right, Johnson, we've got mounts picked out for you and Martinez. Jenkins will tally 'em to you as you need 'em."

"Fine!" Bret said loudly. "Just so they aren't too bronky."

The boys loitered a little longer, shaking out sweat-caked saddle blankets, after the rest had gone on to wash for supper.

"Do you think this Wide Mouth is the same one who offered to sell beef to Otto?" Ace asked.

"I'd bet on it. But we need Otto to identify him."

"How about a picture?" Ace suggested. "I can draw one for Otto to look at."

"That's a top-hand idea, my friend," Bret agreed. "Do you think Wide Mouth was really interested in that Brahma I dropped, or did he reach for it out of curiosity?"

"I don't know," Ace replied. "But he sure wanted it."

"There's the supper gong." Bret tossed his saddle blanket on the fence. "I'm glad rustler hunting doesn't hurt my appetite. We'd better hurry and wash up, *Jake*."

It was a typical, hearty cow-ranch meal: roast beef in gravy, sourdough biscuits, pinto beans boiled with chunks of dried salt pork, canned corn, stewed prunes, and coffee black enough to repaint a faded crow.

For several of the cowboys, this day's riding had been their first experience with wild cattle. So a number of them interrupted eating to tell tall tales of the day's excitement.

Except for Bret's one "big windy" about a wild steer that climbed a tree and kicked his hat off when he rode under it, both Bret and Ace kept quiet.

So, they noticed, did Wide Mouth Williams.

In the bunkhouse after supper Ace got out his sketch pad and pencil, while Bret relaxed with a detective story. Some of the others played pitch, casino, and dominoes.

Sitting on the side of his bunk, Wide Mouth produced a huge harmonica. It was by far the bulkiest mouth harp Bret had ever laid eyes on. It looked to be a very expensive instrument, but the tunes Williams played were the low-grade variety that cowboys call "blow-suck" music.

After a while Wide Mouth put away his harmonica. Moving silently in his sock feet, he came over to sit beside Ace. For a moment he stared

"What about the black Brahma bull?" whispered
Wide Mouth

down at the sketch of a horse on Ace's pad. Then, after a furtive look around the bunkhouse, he stopped and whispered to the Indian.

"Listen, kid—what do you know about the black Brahma bull?"

Casually Ace sketched a small outline of a Brahma. "Bull is nice design for a bolero tie clasp," he said. "I've made many of them—silver, turquoise, black. I'll make you one someday maybe."

"Yeah," grunted Williams, a puzzled look on his face. "Yeah, I'd like that."

Before returning to his bunk he stopped beside Bret who looked up from his book.

Williams was awkward and uncomfortable. "Sometimes I get mad too easy," he blurted out. "Almost killed a man that way once. About this morning—I guess I jumped you out of turn, huh?"

"You're mixed up," said Bret. "I jumped you— for a reason," he added dryly. "Forget it."

After Williams returned to his bunk, Bret casually wandered over for a look at Ace's drawings. On the pad was a sketch of a horse so perfectly done that Bret immediately recognized Shogood. From beneath this paper Ace pulled out a comic sketch of Bret racing Daybreak after a steer.

"If I could draw like that—" Bret began, then stopped short as Ace slid a third sketch from under the first two. It was a likeness of Wide Mouth

Williams, so accurate that it made Bret draw a deep breath of astonishment.

Ace glanced at his friend, an unspoken question in his eyes. Bret nodded. Otto certainly could confirm an identification from this drawing. But getting to Tovar with it was another problem.

The next morning Bret sidled up to Bill Evans who was giving instructions to the cook in the kitchen.

After drawing Bill aside, Bret told him about the picture of Wide Mouth. "If you let me off after work this evening," the boy said, "I'll take the sketch to Otto Mueller."

"Go ahead," Evans agreed. "Better use one of the ranch pickups, so it will look as if you're on an errand for me."

"Thanks," said Bret, and he went to saddle up for the day's work.

The horse Jenkins assigned him that morning was a quiet sorrel called Bug. But when the crew changed mounts at noon at the holding pasture corral, the gray horse that Bret drew was skittish and saddle-shy.

To Bret's surprise, Williams offered to help hold the snorting gray while Bret got the saddle on him. Cowboys figure to ask for help when they need it, and Bret did not welcome this uninvited aid. At the moment it seemed wise not to object, even though Bret had a queer feeling of misgiving.

Together they saddled the horse. But when Bret straddled him, the big mount came unwound in a wild spell of frantic rearing and bucking.

He "pawed the moon," bucked high behind, and came down stiff-legged in front. He zigged, zagged, twisted, whirled in the air, and "stood on his tail."

"Ride him, cowboy!" yelled one of the hands.

"Wa-hoo!" squalled another. "Hang and rattle, cowboy! I'll hold your hat!"

CHAPTER XII

Branding a Braggart

BRET's hat flew off. Six inches of daylight showed between his pants seat and the saddle. He came down in it, but it was like a sledge hammer driving his backbone up into his neck. The bronc spun twice around, bucked high again. Bret felt himself losing his balance. One more whirl would land him in the dust!

With a desperate gathering of every muscle, Bret strained to regain the saddle—and at that instant the gray stopped bucking.

The bronc stood head down, spraddle-legged, trembling all over. Bret knew that unless the foreman Jenkins had deliberately put him on a bronc there must be something the matter with the animal. No usable cow horse would ever put on such a wild wingding without a reason.

Bret dismounted quickly. He stood beside the trembling horse a moment, one hand stroking the

103

gray's sweat-soaked neck. "Poor ol' feller!" he said soothingly. "What's hurting you?"

He unbuckled the cinch and eased off the saddle. Instantly the horse shook himself with relief.

"Oh, oh," Bret said to himself. "I have a hunch what caused this—Williams." He ran his hand under the saddle blanket until it touched a cluster of thorny sandburs.

Bret remembered that burring a saddle blanket was an old cowboy trick sometimes played on new cow hands to test them or put on a show. But it was a trick Bret despised. For the rider it did not matter much. But for a cow horse taught to trust the man on his back, it was nothing less than cruel torture.

Wide Mouth Williams was starting to mount his horse a short distance away.

"Just a minute, Williams!" Bret said sharply, and started toward him, Ace at his side.

Evans was there too. His hand on Bret's arm stopped the boy. "I wouldn't," Bill said quietly. "One more fight, and I'd be obliged to fire you both—like I promised."

From the steady look in Evans' eyes, Bret understood: firing him or firing Williams now would upset the applecart so far as their rustler sleuthing was concerned.

"You're the boss, Mr. Evans," Bret said.

One of the cow hands, a ruddy-cheeked, cotton-topped cowboy called Whitey, whacked Bret on the back. "Maybe I've seen smoother bronc rides, cowboy." He laughed. "Anyhow, you was still on top when the wind quit blowin'! That's what counts."

Whitey's friendly joshing helped cool Bret's wrath, and he responded with a good-natured grin.

"Old Graybill sure gave me a good view of the country," he said. "That's the highest I've sailed since I rode a Ferris wheel at the fair!"

"All right, boys!" Evans called out sternly, becoming impatient over the delay. "Let's get at it!"

Bret did not ask for a new mount. With Ace to help hold the still-nervous gray, he eased the saddle on, cinched up, and mounted. He lifted the bridle reins and applied the spurs gently.

The horse rolled his eyes and snuffed a little. Then, with the sandburs no longer hurting him, he seemed to remember that he was a cow horse with a cowboy on his back. The gray trotted out of the corral, ears alert, and ready for work.

A dozen other cow hands straddled eager horseflesh and loped out to start gathering cattle. Bill Evans had named the day's work, and no further orders were needed. Even this miscellaneous crew of drifters knew what to do.

The holding pasture—which cow people call a "trap"—was not more than a couple of hundred acres. Rounding up the batch of steers in it and crowding them into the stout-fenced branding corral took no more than half an hour.

In one end of the corral Bill Evans already had the branding irons heated to the proper cherry red in a modern gasoline-torch iron heater. On a nearby shelf on the fence, dehorning saws and big vaccination needles lay ready, along with the "dope bucket"—a pail of sticky, tarlike medicine to be swabbed on the wounds of dehorning.

To the riders now gathered inside the pen, Evans briefly assigned individual duties: which ones to rope, which to "tail down" and hold the steers, which to saw off horns.

Jenkins would boss the dehorning; Evans himself handle the irons and hypodermic needles.

Pete Kyler, the kid of the outfit, automatically drew the messy job of handling the dope bucket.

With all duties covered, two men were without jobs. To these Evans said, "Murphy, you and Spike go ride the north beef pasture. Take your six-shooters. Any truck rustlers you catch, shoot 'em and bring me their ears!"

The last was said with a dry grin, and Evans added, "I don't want thieves sneaking in on us while we're busy working these steers. All right, boys! Let's fly at it!"

Bret and Ace were pleased that Evans had teamed them together for roping. But Bret wondered about assigning Wide Mouth Williams to rope with Whitey Gibbs. He had overheard Wide Mouth bragging about what a top-hand roper he was. Yet there was something about the way Williams sat heavy in the saddle that made Bret doubt whether he was as much of a cow hand as he pretended to be.

"Why do you suppose Evans assigned Williams to rope?" asked Bret, as he and Ace slacked out their own loops.

"Best cure for big brag," said Ace, "is make him prove it."

Quickly Ace dabbed a neat loop over a rangy steer's horns, turned his horse, and started dragging the steer toward the branding fire. Bret rode behind the critter, whipping him along with his rope. The steer lunged and plunged this way and that, but Ace's horse kept the rope tight. The steer had to come.

As soon as Ace got the animal within a few yards of the branding station, Bret's loop flipped down and picked up the animal's heels. The next second the boys had the steer stretched out between their two horses pulling in opposite directions.

The stretch alone would have downed the Chihuahua in a moment. But to make him fall on the right side, so that the brand could be burned on his left hip, a cowboy on foot grabbed the tail and yanked him over.

The instant the steer hit the ground, two cowboys got on his head. One twisted it back to hold him down. The other removed Ace's rope to make room for sawing the horns off close.

Already the acrid smoke of burning hair was curling up from the red-hot iron Evans pressed briefly to the steer's hip. By the time Evans swapped his branding iron for a hypodermic needle and injected the dose of combined serums under the loose skin of the steer's neck, Jenkins had one horn sawed off. Then the range boss sawed off the other horn, and Ky swabbed both stubs.

In scarcely two minutes the triple job was done, the steer turned loose, and the ropers on their way after another beast.

Now was the moment when Williams and Whitey should be arriving with another steer. Instead, Wide Mouth had tossed a "washerwoman" loop that snagged two steers at once. He and Whitey were having a ruckus trying to get the mess untangled.

Bret could have helped them, but he knew the custom of the branding pen: every man must handle his own job—unless there was danger of someone's getting hurt.

Bret and Ace had delivered another steer and

Bret whipped the steer along with his rope

were starting back for their third when Whitey finally came up dragging a Chihuahua to the fire. Williams missed the steer's heels twice, then picked up only one foot with his next loop. The tailers flopped him anyhow, and the ground crew worked him. But Whitey's face was red with wrath.

"How about this, Bill?" he called to Evans. "Hasn't this outfit got any ropers?"

"I heard somewhere that you were a roper, Williams," Evans said quietly. "Get down and see if you know how to grab a steer's tail. Romero, you rope with Whitey."

Wide Mouth swore under his breath, but he obeyed. He did so poorly at tailing and holding that within ten minutes Evans had downgraded him to the dope bucket, much to Pete Kyler's joy. From then on the work went smoothly.

That evening at supper Williams ate in surly silence. He left the table before the others and went outside. Bret had seen him look surreptitiously at his watch. Now, on a hunch, Bret stepped outside in the shadow of a trumpet vine to watch where Wide Mouth went.

He saw Williams stroll casually across the yard, then suddenly hurry up to the top of a nearby little knoll. There he sat down on a rock and began playing his big harmonica.

At that instant Bret heard the hum of an airplane motor. On another sudden hunch he ran to the bunkhouse for his binoculars.

He was too late with the glasses, but by the naked-eye glimpse he got of the plane, it looked like the same one that had flown Dr. Dudley into Oro Perdido Canyon.

"What do you make of it, Ace?" he asked his Indian pal who had followed him out.

"I watched." Ace shook his head. "Williams made no signal."

"Maybe we're just jittery." Bret folded the sketch of Williams that Ace had drawn the night before, got into a Flying Spur pickup truck, and headed out for his errand in Tovar.

Darkness overtook him within a few miles. Only then was he aware of the lights of a car following him.

When he sped up, the other car sped up. When Bret slowed down, it slowed down. Finally Bret's speedometer dropped to twenty-five miles an hour, and to his relief the trailing black sedan passed him.

All the way to Tovar, Bret pondered the driver's strange behavior. Was the fellow merely timid, or was he following Bret's movements? And if the latter were true, who had found out about his plans?

The boy was doubly cautious as he stopped in front of Mueller's butcher shop. It was closed, but there was a light in Otto's quarters upstairs. Bret slid out of the truck, whistled, and called, "Hey, Otto!"

Suddenly something hit him hard on the head. Bret slumped to the ground, knocked out cold.

When Bret came to, Otto was dashing water into his face. "What happened? Come. I help you upstairs."

The boy rose, rubber-legged, leaned on Otto, and staggered to the butcher's quarters. Seated in Otto's rocking chair, and still dizzy, he felt for his wallet. It was gone—and Ace's sketch of Wide Mouth with it.

"Now I have spilled the beans!" Bret thought. *"If the sneak who knocked me out is in cahoots with Williams, he'll tip off that wide-mouthed critter who I am and they may guess my real business at the Flying Spur!"*

CHAPTER XIII

Night Riders

Otto applied a cold pack of folded towel to the bump rising on Bret's head, and laid out some clean cotton strips and salve for a bandage. Then he hustled downstairs and returned with something on a plate.

"Here! Eat this knockwurst, my boy!" he urged. "It is the best thing to restore your strength."

Despite his throbbing head, Bret had to laugh at the idea of sausage as a quick restorative. But to please the butcher he ate some.

"Thank you," he said. "I feel better already."

"Just after you whistled," Otto told him, "I heard a car make a quick leave-away."

"Maybe the car that passed me on the road *did* have me spotted," Bret thought. Aloud he said, "My wallet has been stolen. I'd better phone Sheriff Buxton."

Bret's legs were still a little wobbly, but he made

it down to the butcher shop where the phone was located.

Andy answered.

"This is Bret. I—"

"Well, howdy, boy!" Andy's drawl broke in. "I thought you went buckaroostering over on the Spur."

"I did. But right now I'm at Otto Mueller's with no wallet and a lump on my head. I want to talk with your dad."

"Sorry, Bret." Andy's voice sobered. "There's been a big bank holdup at Plateau City and Dad's out on a roadblock. They think the bandits got away in a stolen car. If you have any secrets, you can tell 'em to ol' Andy."

"I'll do that, Texas boy," Bret said dryly. "But not over the telephone."

"I was just leaving for Vic's house," Andy went on. "Mr. Martinson's all steamed up about the bank robberies. Can you meet me there right away?"

"Will do. Pronto!" Bret agreed.

After Bret had thanked Otto he returned to his truck and in a few minutes was at the Martinson home.

Orvel Martinson, president of the Tovar Stockmen's Bank, lived in a two-story house of red brick, rather imposing but conservative. The driveway light was on and Vic was at the door when

Bret arrived. Andy had just stepped off his motor-cycle which was parked beside the garage.

The boys hurried into the living room, where Mr. Martinson rose to greet them. He was a stocky man with a ruddy face and blond hair. As soon as Bret and Andy had said a polite good evening, the banker took them into his study with Vic.

"Boys," he said, "this epidemic of bold, rash bank robberies has me worried. The criminals may try Tovar next."

"They'd better not," Andy said grimly. "Dad will be ready for them."

"They may be brazen enough to try," Mr. Martinson ventured.

"Or stupid enough," Andy countered, "because their *modus operandi* is always the same."

"You're right," the executive agreed. "Some-where the thieves are obtaining nerve gas. They enter a bank, slip on gas masks, fire a nerve-gas gun—sometimes two of them—and knock every-body out cold. Then they gather up the money and make their getaway."

"The nerve gas only paralyzes for a few min-utes," Vic added, "but by the time the people in the bank recover, the robbers are gone, and the alarm is spread too late."

"Sheriff Buxton and the State Police seem to be doing everything they can," Martinson went on. "But I have a suggestion. I'd like the sheriff to deputize two or three men to guard the Stockmen's Bank. Of course I'd stand any expense."

"Good men for deputies are about as scarce around here as hair on a Texas horned toad," Andy said. "But I know Dad will find 'em for you if he can. Maybe we could even supply them with gas masks."

"That certainly would be appreciated." Martinson looked at his watch. "Now, if you boys will excuse me, I have a meeting to attend. Please make yourselves at home. I believe Mrs. Martinson has some fresh doughnuts and lemonade she'd like to get rid of." He shook hands with Bret and Andy, then left.

Alone with his two chums, Bret told what had happened during the past two days, adding, "This egg on my noggin is the latest souvenir."

"Well, one thing sure," Andy commented. "Williams isn't a cowboy or he'd know how to rope."

Mrs. Martinson, a slender, gracious woman, came in with a tray of doughnuts, glasses, and a pitcher of lemonade.

While the boys enjoyed the refreshments, Andy said he also had a report to make.

"I rode the Oro Perdido side of the Rimrock yesterday," he said, "and spied on the Ortega place. The Dudley-Colfax outfit seemed to be busy."

"Doing what?" Bret asked.

"I couldn't make out what they were up to,"

Andy confessed. "Then Dad sent for me to cover the office. So I came back without any real clues." He paused and added, "A little while ago Jinx called me from the ranch. Hey, we didn't come out even! Who gets the last doughnut?"

"Never mind the doughnut!" Bret exclaimed. "What did Jinx have to say?"

"Rusty and Jinx were up on the mesa just at dark," Andy went on, taking the doughnut. "They saw a lot of strange lights down in the Oro Perdido —looked like *electric* lights, Jinx said."

"So we pile on another mystery!" Bret remarked. "How many does that make?" Without waiting for an answer, he declared, "By golly, let's go take a look for ourselves—right now—tonight!"

"You mean ride up that rocky trail to this side of the canyon in the dark?" Vic asked incredulously. "You know I'm not so good a rider as you fellows."

"Let the horse worry about that," Bret told him. "He'll follow the trail. All you have to do is hang on. Now about horses—"

"We can use ours," Vic offered quickly. "Dad had them shod just a few days ago. But won't it be terribly slow on horseback all the way from here? Perhaps we could take the horses part way in a trailer."

"But who's got a three-horse trailer?" Andy asked, munching the last bite of doughnut.

"My Flying Spur pickup is rigged to haul a horse," Bret said. "That's one. If Mr. Martinson will let us take his two-horse trailer and ranch wagon—"

"For the important business we have, I won't even have to ask him," Vic assured them.

"We can drive on the old Chamisal Road as far as the Table Rocks." Bret laid out the plan. "Then ride on from there."

Orvel Martinson often took his horses on hunting or camping trips, so they were used to being hauled. It did not take long to load them, even in the dark.

The little-used Chamisal Road was badly washed out and rough. Bret made it without trouble in the pickup, but two horses in a trailer made a heavy drag on the power of Vic's ranch wagon. Five miles from their destination, it stalled in a sandy arroyo. At the same time, streaks of lightning started to tear jagged rips in a cloud bank on the horizon.

"Now what do we do?" asked Vic, still inexperienced in the rough-and-ready ways of the cow country. He had heard about flash floods that sometimes roar down dry arroyos, even from a distant cloudburst.

"Don't worry," said Andy. He rummaged behind the seat and came up with a tow chain. "Standard equipment in the Southwest," he said.

Soon he and Bret had hooked the stalled ranch

wagon to the pickup and pulled it on across the arroyo.

They reached the place called Table Rocks without further trouble. There they unloaded the horses, adjusted cinches, mounted, and struck out for the Oro Perdido rim.

The tortuous trail was steep, rocky, and snaggy with overgrown brush. The fact that the Martinson horses had never been on it before put the burden of guiding on Bret. Luckily the young cowboy knew every foot of his home country, in daylight or dark.

A hundred yards from the top of the ridge, Bret reined up.

"Funny thing," he said, "sounds like somebody whistling, but I can't tell where it comes from."

Neither could the others.

"Maybe it's one of Rusty's ghosts," Andy remarked, and they rode on.

A polished white moon broke free of clouds, flooding the night with a pale, eerie light. For the last dozen yards the rock-cluttered trail was almost straight up. Topping the rim, the riders paused to let their horses catch their wind, then rode across the narrow ridgetop to the rim above Oro Perdido Canyon.

"Wow!" breathed Bret. "Look at that!"

Down in the canyon the glitter of a whole galaxy of electric lights brightened the area. Out along the long flat below the Ortega house, glow-ing red and green markers outlined what could be meant only for an airstrip.

"Now why would anybody want to fly in here at night?" Bret wondered aloud. "Listen!"

The drone of a plane echoed against the canyon walls, but the boys could see no lights. Almost immediately the craft switched on landing lights, then glided down on the flat. In a few moments the boys could make out three men unloading bulky cargo from the fuselage.

"There's something rotten in Denmark!" Vic said excitedly. "I'm going to get a better look."

As he stepped off his horse and started down to a jutting ledge of the rimrock a few yards below, a flashlight dropped from his pocket. Before Vic could stoop to pick it up, the flashlight started rolling down the hill. The bumping jarred its switch on, and it lodged against a scrub-oak snag, its glare pointed straight down into the valley.

"Douse it, quick, before they spot us!" Bret warned.

As Vic started for the flashlight, from somewhere in the moon shadows came the whirring warning of a rattlesnake!

CHAPTER XIV

Whistling Bullets

VIC MARTINSON froze in his tracks, unable to locate the deadly buzz. Bret's ears were better trained for such sounds.

"Vic! Don't move an inch!" he ordered quietly. "Let the flashlight go. That's just about where the snake is."

Vic obeyed. Bret and Andy dismounted swiftly. Both of them whizzed fist-sized rocks past Vic at the same instant. One of them put out the flashlight.

The snake rattled again. Bret heaved a larger rock in the direction of the sound and the buzzing stopped.

"Vic," Bret said in the same quiet tone, "take a long, quick step uphill—and come on up here—fast!"

Vic was shaky when he returned to his horse,

but the excitement was not over. Suddenly flashes of orange flame winked from below. The crack of shots and the whine of bullets glancing off nearby rocks came almost at once. The trio pressed themselves to the ground until the firing ceased.

"It looks as if Dudley, Colfax, and Company mean business," Bret commented. "They had a good bead on that flashlight. But they won't chase us," Bret reasoned, "because they don't know how to get here, especially in the dark."

"Sometimes I wish I'd stayed in Texas," Andy said calmly. "Let's watch these buckaroos awhile longer."

The boys moved at a crouch to the canyon rim a few yards from where the flashlight had dropped. In the shadow of a clumpy juniper, they looked over the rim just in time to see the unlighted plane take off, looking like a huge dark bird in the misty moonglow.

After the roar of its motor had died, Bret was aware of the *put-put* sound of a smaller motor. It seemed to come from a shed back of the Ortega house that Colfax and Dudley had taken over.

"An electric generator!"

"Sounds like a diesel," Andy added.

The airstrip lights winked out, but nothing else happened.

As they went back to their horses, Bret noticed that the breeze had freshened, accompanied again by the eerie whistling sound they had heard earlier.

"It's the wind whipping over one of those crazy chimney rocks," Bret surmised.

"Like blowing across the top of a pop bottle," Andy remarked. "Gosh, I'm thirsty."

As the trio mounted, Vic said, "We came, we saw, we got shot at. *Quo vademus?*"

"If that's Latin for where do we go from here," Bret suggested, "let's go take a look at the cliff dwellings and see if those alleged archaeologists have actually done any excavating."

The way around the ridge to the cliff dwellings was not far, but the going was rough. Once more Vic marveled at Bret's ability to pick his way in the darkness.

They found the old ruins more extensive than Bret had realized, but could see no sign of any archaeological digging. The trail up from the Ortega place, however, had been freshly repaired and cleared of loose rock, as if somebody expected to use it often.

"We'll have to come back and really explore this place," Bret remarked.

"Sure is spooky," Andy commented. "I don't blame the Ortegas for believing it's haunted."

"A thousand years ago," Vic said in his thoughtful way, "the same moon shone here upon the peaceful sleep of a now-vanished people."

"Speaking of sleep," Bret yawned, "I was out roping steers at sunup this morning. I could use a little slumber."

The route down to the flats was breath-taking and rapid, and the boys reached their cars quickly. Andy drove the pickup, and Bret snoozed most of the way to town.

In Tovar they helped Vic put up the horses. Then Bret went to spend what little was left of the night with Andy.

At dawn the sheriff called them to breakfast. Over ham and eggs, Bret discussed the situation with Buxton.

"Nobody hit you on the head just for practice," the sheriff told him. "There's a tie-up in all this skulduggery somewhere. We can arrest Williams for questioning, if you think we should."

"No, Sheriff," Bret said after a moment's thought. "We still lack the kind of concrete evidence we need. There's no proof that Williams had anything to do with last night. Besides, we want Wide Mouth *loose,* as a possible lead to the rest of the gang."

"Right, my boy," the sheriff agreed. "And in that case, I expect you'd better be getting on back to the Flying Spur."

Bret drove off a few minutes later. Arriving at the Spur shortly after sunrise, he found the whole place in an uproar, and Bill Evans furious.

"What happened?" Bret asked.

"Fences cut and two steers butchered on the spot," the manager stormed. "We don't know how many others were hauled away alive last night,"

Evans continued grimly. "How they knew where to strike so as to miss our patrols sure enough beats me!"

Evans paused as he saw Ace, Ky, and Whitey hurrying excitedly toward him.

"Well, boys, what's up now?"

"Williams has lit a shuck!" Ky blurted out.

"Apparently sneaked out before daylight," Whitey reported. "Paisano is missing, and so is my .30-30."

"That doggoned critter would steal the fastest-traveling horse on the ranch!" Evans exploded bitterly. "With the head start he's got, Paisano will make him hard to catch. Who's a good tracker around here?"

"Jake could track a tick on a tin roof," Bret told him, indicating Ace.

"Just a minute!" Whitey said. "Where were you last night, fellow?" He pointed to Bret.

"He was on an errand for me." Evans spoke up quickly. "He's okay. Take it from me, we can trust Johnson. I'm going tracking with Martinez, Johnson, and Ky," he continued. "Jenkins has plenty here to keep you busy, Whitey. You saddle up while I notify the sheriff," he added, and Ky, Ace, and Bret quickly obeyed.

Horse tracks on a cow ranch are usually thicker than spots on a speckled trout. But from the maze of tracks coming and going, Ace soon sorted out the right one.

Not only was it fresh, but once it got well away from the corrals, Evans identified Paisano's long stride and the print of number-one shoes with a slight turn-in on the left hoof.

At first Williams had ridden at an easy gait, evidently to avoid suspicion if his departure was noticed. But once beyond a low hill, out of sight of the ranch, he had put Paisano to a hard gallop. The hoofs had churned up sod and sand enough to make the tracks easy to follow for two or three miles.

After that, Williams had apparently slowed down and begun to fox his trail by taking a zigzag course up and down the many little rock-ribbed ridges where even an iron horseshoe would leave no track.

"The fellow is smarter than I expected," Ace commented. "Maybe we won't catch him after all."

Following the tracks now became a slow and laborious job, but to Ace's keen eyes even the smallest scuff on a rock was enough.

"I believe ol' Ace smells those tracks, like a bloodhound," Bret commented.

"Don't have to smell." Ace grinned. "Indians know how to look."

While Ace kept his eyes on the ground, the other three scanned the country for sign of the fugitive. Bill Evans carried a .30-30 across his saddle, and Bret had no doubt that he meant to use it if necessary. But they sighted no horseman.

Around midmorning Bill's horse threw a shoe. "This rocky footing will lame a barefoot horse mighty quick," he said. "I'll have to quit you and turn back. You'd better take this," he added, handing his rifle to Bret. "You may need it. Good luck."

Bret took the .30-30 but hoped he would not have to use it. He had never pointed a weapon at a human being in his life.

Bret, Ace, and Ky continued the chase. Mile after mile the boys followed Ace's lead, their horses sweat-lathered in the hot sun.

Finally they crossed a draw with water in it. Bret did not need Ace to read sign for him here. From the shallowness of tracks in the mud where

Williams had let Paisano stop to drink, it was plain that the horse had stood there only a moment.

"That means Wide Mouth knew better than to let his horse fill up," Ace commented. "He knows more about horses than I figured."

They allowed their own horses only a few sips, knowing that too much water in the belly of an overheated horse is bad for traveling.

The search continued, slowly but thoroughly. Trying to fox his trail, Williams had ridden into a scrub-oak thicket, then out again almost immediately. It was here that Ky "hit pay dirt."

"Look! There's Williams' slicker!" he exclaimed, breathless with excitement.

In his hurry to get away, the fugitive had failed to tie the raincoat securely behind the saddle, and the oak brush had snagged it off.

Without waiting for Bret and Ace, Ky spurred his horse up the hill to get the slicker.

"From the general course Wide Mouth is taking," Bret reasoned while they waited for Ky, "it looks as if he's headed for the Oro Perdido."

Suddenly Ky let out an excited shout. They saw him pick up the slicker, and something else. Then he came back to them at a lope, with Williams' harmonica held high.

"Look, fellows!" Ky yelled. "It's not just a mouth harp! *It's got a built-in radio!*"

CHAPTER XV

A Futile Search

"WELL, I'll be a burro's uncle!" exclaimed Bret, examining the compact receiver and transmitter. "See what Williams was up to? He's been tipping off the rustlers with this camouflaged radio."

"Pretty clever," Ace said, and recalled Wide Mouth's trip to the hilltop the evening before. "He must have signaled the plane as it flew over."

"Hey! Look at this!" Bret had been examining the slicker. *Inside a pocket was a duplicate of the black obsidian Brahma bull Bret had picked up at the wrecked truck!*

"I told you that bull meant something," Ace said.

"But what? Those rustlers have us going in circles!"

"Go in circles long enough," Ace observed sagely, "and you'll find what's in the middle."

"We won't find any middle sitting here palavering," said Ky. "Let's chase after Williams before he gets clear to Arizona!"

"Right!" Bret agreed.

He rolled the harmonica-radio carefully in Wide Mouth's slicker, and tied it on his saddle. Again they set out on the fugitive's trail.

Bill Evans had been right about the stolen horse being a good traveler. Mile after long mile they followed the long-strided tracks. Their own horses began to show signs of tiredness. But still they caught no glimpse of Williams.

When the fugitive's trail definitely lined out in the direction of Rimrock Ranch, Bret spoke his conclusion:

"He's heading for the Oro Perdido, all right. That may tie up the package for us, proving at least that Dudley and Colfax are mixed up in this."

But on that score Williams fooled them all. If Dudley and Colfax were indeed his pals, as Bret suspected, Wide Mouth apparently did not mean to give away that fact by leading his pursuers to the Ortega place.

Instead, the boys found that he had passed within half a mile of the Rimrock headquarters, apparently headed for the high country beyond.

"Fellows," Bret suggested, "with the head start Williams has, we won't catch him right quick. Let's stop at the ranch, pick up fresh horses and some chow. We may be on this trail a long time."

The Kings were surprised when the trio rode in on sweaty Flying Spur horses. Andy, Vic, Benny, and Big Jim had just returned from scouting the steer pastures. But none of them had sighted Williams.

"I'm going to call Sheriff Buxton," Bret said. "He'll want to meet us and tail Williams."

But when Bret phoned Tovar he was dismayed to find that both the sheriff and his chief deputy had been summoned early that morning by State Police in Santa Fe.

"They're having a big powwow, trying to figure how to nab those bank robbers," Bret reported when he returned.

Big Jim had no news to report, but Vic and Andy had cleared up one small puzzle.

"We found out whose car made the tracks where the gate was left open and the colt got cut," Andy told Bret. "We can check that off."

"It was Luke Higgins—that old photographer in Tovar," Vic explained. "He was out taking scenic pictures for post cards."

Andy chuckled. "We nearly scared him to death when we identified the car tracks and chewed him out about it."

"He ought to have his pants kicked for leaving the gate open," Big Jim put in. "But he's not mixed up in any monkey business. Everybody knows old Luke is harmless as a kitten—except he's absent-minded."

By the time Bret, Ace, and Ky had eaten a solid meal, Big Jim, Andy, Benny, Vic, and Rusty were all ready and eager to trail the rustlers' spy.

At first Big Jim said Rusty would have to stay at home, but when Bret put in a good word for the boy, his father relented.

"But you can't ride out on one of those midget mustangs," Bret told him. "If Williams is headed for the timber country, you'll need a horse with legs long enough to step over logs."

"That's all right." Rusty grinned happily. "I'd ride an ol' giraffe to go with you."

"Boys," said Big Jim, "with renegades running loose and this smell of danger in the air, we mustn't leave the women here alone. One of us will have to stay with them."

After some discussion, Big Jim reluctantly agreed to be the one to stay. Though Mrs. King and Jinx both had protested that they did not need a guardian, Bret could see that his mother was relieved by the decision.

The expanded posse mounted fresh horses and set out after Williams again.

"Well, gee my wheeze!" Benny grinned. "Seven coyotes after one rabbit!" But he knew as well as the others that Wide Mouth was a dangerous character.

As they followed the fugitive's tracks, Bret's surmise proved to be right. Wide Mouth's trail led over the mesa, into piny foothills, then up a long canyon into the high country. The sun had already begun to cast long shadows when they reached the upper ridges, thickly forested with pine and fir and white-trunked aspen.

The fact that Paisano had been able to carry Williams so far was amazing. Now the tracks, however, began to show the drag of fatigue. Every now and then Williams had stopped to let the horse rest. In some places he had even walked and led his mount.

"It's a good thing he's following a trail," Ace commented, as the posse pressed on mile after mile of hard climbing. "In the shadow of the timber, tracks are hard to see."

This was a trail Bret and his friends had often ridden together. It led to a good trout stream, hidden deep in the mountains. Riding it now on such a grim errand gave Bret a strange feeling of unreality. Yet he well knew how desperately real the clash with an armed outlaw could be, once they overtook him.

Topping a broad, aspen-groved mountain, they suddenly saw a she-bear with two coal-black cubs amble across the trail. The sight, and more particularly the scent, spooked the horses. Those in the lead, snorted, reared, lunged around, and tried to turn back.

Rusty's mount bucked but the boy stayed aboard. When the horse quieted, however, Rusty was sitting behind the saddle on the horse's rump.

"Now that's what I like to see," Bret teased him, "a cowboy who can ride all over the horse!"

The brief excitement served to relieve the nervous tension of expecting at any moment to come upon the outlaw or be shot at from ambush.

At evening they still had not overtaken their man. As twilight shadows closed in on them, Ace finally lost Williams' trail. But there was still no thought of giving up the chase.

"There's a spring and some little grassy glades up the trail a piece," Bret told Vic. "We'll have to risk camping for the night."

They dismounted under the spreading branches

of a big Engelmann's spruce near one of the little glades Bret had mentioned. The area, a relic of an old forest fire, was cluttered with dead logs and snags, but there was a little grass in it for the horses.

Unsaddling, they hobbled four of the horses and turned them loose in the glade. Vic's horse, a gentle bay named Goody, and two others were allowed to roam.

"I know these ponies," Bret assured Vic. "Those three won't leave the others."

With no fire, lest it betray their camp, no bedding, and only cold biscuits to eat, they spent a shivery night.

Anxious to make himself useful, Rusty hurried out at the first crack of dawn to start catching the horses. As he headed across the glade to bridle his own horse first, he caught a glimpse of the Goody bay disappearing into the timber.

Thinking the horse had started to stray, Rusty hit a high lope across the glade and into the woods after the animal.

Bret and Ace came into the clearing too late to see Rusty vanish. But the Navajo quickly found his footprints. He also discovered Goody's tracks—and those of a man leading the horse!

"Williams!"

"Surely Rusty would have called if he'd seen him," Bret said. "He's got more sense than to follow him alone."

At that moment Rusty's high-pitched cry came from deep in the timber.

"Bret! Help! He's—" The words choked off.

As Bret and Ace started toward the cry, a man's voice called out hoarsely: "Stay back! Come another step and you'll never see this kid again!"

Both cowboys froze in their tracks.

CHAPTER XVI

S O S

Out of sight in a nearby loggy glade, Williams was having his own troubles. Trying to hold Rusty with one hand, he reached for a rope with the other. Frantic to escape, Rusty stamped on Wide Mouth's right foot, kicked his other shin, and gave him a shove. Caught off balance, Wide Mouth sprawled across a log.

"Come back, you young polecat! Stop or I'll shoot!" Wide Mouth thundered. Scrambling to his feet he snatched his rifle from its saddle sheath.

Swift as a cat, Rusty leaped on Vic's bay horse, yanked him around, and dug in his heels. As the bay ran, Rusty swung himself low on one side, Indian style, as Ace had taught him.

Wham! The man's shot missed the running target.

A moment later Rusty was back with Bret and

Ace. His brother wasted no time in scolding. Quickly he gave the boys directions how to spread out and surround the outlaw.

"Ace and I will handle him," he said. "But be ready to rush in to help if we need it."

A few minutes later Wide Mouth, crouched behind a big fallen log, heard the whistling calls of camp-robber jays on both sides of him. Williams was not woodsman enough to recognize the signals by which Bret and Ace kept each other located as they slowly crept up on their prey.

Suddenly Bret sprang out and leaped at the outlaw. With a startled oath, Wide Mouth swung around, pointing his rifle directly at Bret!

As Williams' finger reached the trigger, Ace sprang swiftly as a panther and landed on the man's back.

The rifle cracked, but the aim was wild. Before Wide Mouth could squeeze off a second shot, Bret wrenched the .30-30 from his grasp, and Ace's strong brown fingers were around the outlaw's throat, clamping hard on the whiskery man's oversized Adam's apple.

Bret had never seen his Navajo friend so intensely angry.

"Easy does it, Ace," he admonished. "We want this man to be able to talk."

"You're my friend," Ace said. "He tried to kill you!" Nevertheless, he loosened his grip, as Andy, Vic, Ky, Benny, and Rusty gathered around.

"Well, gee my wheeze!" exclaimed Benny. "I thought for sure somebody got shot."

"I would have been if it hadn't been for Ace," Bret said. "Now let's saddle up and deliver this varmint to the sheriff."

"I hope he gets what he deserves," Ky said, "if only for what he's done to a good horse!"

They all turned to look at Paisano. Two days before the chestnut had been a sleek, well-conditioned, alert cow horse. Now he stood gaunt and hollow-flanked, his head low, his ears drooping.

"Williams," Bret said, unable to withhold his contempt, "riding a fine horse almost to death is mighty near as bad as stealing beef!"

Williams made no reply, but gulped and rubbed his neck.

As the lightest load, Rusty rode Paisano and Bret put Williams on Rusty's horse for the return trip. He lashed Wide Mouth's hands together to the saddle horn, then led the horse. Through it all, Williams wore his bushy eyebrows in a scowl and kept his mouth tightly shut.

Big Jim, Mrs. King, and Jinx were excited to see the youthful posse ride in with the glowering prisoner.

"Great work!" the rancher congratulated them. "So this is Wide Mouth Williams!" He pulled the man from his horse, seized his shirt front, and looked him in the eye. "Steal my beef, will you, you low-down coyote!"

"Worse than that, Dad," Rusty said. "He tried to steal Vic's horse and kidnap me and shoot Bret!"

Big Jim's jaw clenched. He shook Williams so hard that the outlaw's head bobbed like a grotesque rag doll's. "I ought to horsewhip you. Who hired you to do this?"

The prisoner stared mutely at the ground.

"Well, Buxton can take over from here," Big Jim said. "Tie him up, Bret, and put him in the truck."

Ace helped with the job and they flopped Williams into the back of the pickup. Bret thanked Ky for his aid, and the wrangler set off for home with the Flying Spur horses, carrying the .30-30 with him.

While Benny stayed behind to tend the ranch, the others drove to Tovar, using both the truck and the Kings' station wagon. When they arrived, Vic hurried home to report the news, and Mrs. King and Jinx went shopping. The rest of the party took Wide Mouth to Sheriff Buxton's office in the courthouse.

"All right, Williams." Buxton took over immediately. "First we'll take your fingerprints and get them to the FBI."

"Go ahead, waste your time!" Williams muttered. "They got nothing on me."

"Williams," Bret began while Andy took the prints, "let's have it straight. We know you're mixed up in this truck rustling. Who is it that's got you over a barrel, making you do the dirty work?"

"Who, me?" Williams looked at once wary and defiant. "I don't know what you're talking about."

"What about that harmonica-radio?"

For a split second the prisoner looked startled. "What do you think you are, kid—the district attorney?"

"Whoever he is," said Sheriff Buxton sternly, "you answer him."

"No soap." Williams shrugged. "I ain't talking. Ask my lawyer."

"You have a lawyer?" Ace asked.

"I'll get one!"

"How about Colfax and Dudley?" Bret asked.

"Never heard of 'em."

For an hour they grilled Williams with every kind of question they could think of—but the net result was zero.

Finally the sheriff said, "If he won't talk, he won't talk. For the present we'll book him for horse stealing and assault with a deadly weapon. Maybe a few days in jail will loosen his tongue."

Returning to his office after locking up Wide Mouth, Sheriff Buxton seemed somewhat encouraged. "Seeing one wolf trapped makes others trapshy," he said. "I've a notion grabbing Williams will stop this rustling—at least for a while."

"But not cure it," Big Jim remarked.

"We have to keep after them," Bret asserted stubbornly. "Besides—"

He broke off abruptly as Jinx hurried into the office, waving a paper in her hand, followed by Vic.

"Look, Bret!" she panted. "It's a letter from Penn's Grove College. They *did* sponsor two archaeologists named Dudley and Colfax for a project in New Mexico."

"That sort of shortens our fish pole," Bret said, disappointed. "Colfax and Dudley—bona fide scientists—" He shook his head.

"I have news, too," said Vic, "about that air-plane. The identification numbers showed it belongs to a charter pilot of Omaha, Nebraska. His name is Ralph Reese. I located his wife Helen and talked to her on long-distance."

Mrs. Reese, Vic reported, said that her husband had left with two men on a charter flight several weeks before. She had not seen him since, but she had received several typewritten letters post-marked Tovar, signed with Reese's name, assuring her that he was all right.

Vic paused, almost breathless with the importance of his information. "Mrs. Reese said the typed letters were not unusual, since Reese had a portable machine with him. But she also said the salutation on the last letter was 'Dear Ellen.' He had never called her by that name before."

"Helen and Ellen do sound alike," Jinx mused. "But I can't imagine a husband getting them mixed up. Maybe someone else is writing the letters!"

"You've got something there, Sis. I've thought all along there was something peculiar about that pilot not getting out of the plane the other day."

"Perhaps I should add," Vic said, "that quite naturally, Mrs. Reese is worried."

"Maybe I can help her," Bret said. He turned to Big Jim. "May I take the pickup? I'd like to get home in time to ride over to the Oro Perdido."

"Sure, Bret. Take Rusty along."

Rusty, who was examining a pair of handcuffs,

quickly came to his brother's side. Vic, Ace, and Andy decided their chores had been so neglected they would have to stay in town.

"It's not that we don't love you, country boy." Andy whacked Bret on the shoulder. "It's just that we're kept busy leading a double life."

As soon as they reached the ranch, Bret and Rusty saddled up and headed for the Oro Perdido. Half a mile out Benny Ortega quit riding range and joined them.

They found the gate to the Ortega property locked and Wiley standing guard with a shotgun. Bret decided the best strategy would be to act innocently polite. "Howdy," he greeted Wiley. "I wonder if we could see Dr. Dudley and Professor Colfax."

"Maybe you punks can't read." Wiley scowled. "The sign says 'No Admittance.' Now beat it!"

"There comes Professor Colfax now," Bret said, and they waited.

This time Colfax did not seem hostile. Even when Bret asked him if, by any chance, his pilot was named Ralph Reese, Colfax showed no emotion.

"Yes, and that's him coming in to land now," he said. Colfax waved his hat as the gray plane taxied to a stop. The pilot, and a man whom the boys recognized as Jones, stepped out and came to the gate.

Reese was a mild-mannered man of about thirty. His large brown eyes had a sad, inquiring look.

"Ralph," Colfax said, "these are a couple of neighbors from the Rimrock Ranch. I guess we didn't act very friendly toward them at first, but that's all in the past, now that we know who they are."

"Mr. Reese," Bret said, "we've heard you're a fine pilot. Could we hire you to take us for a ride one of these days?"

"Well, now, that depends." The pilot stood nervously toeing the dirt. "I'm tied up at present."

"Oh, there's no hurry," Bret assured him genially. "Just sometime when the weather is nice and you aren't busy."

"We know what all this country looks like to a cowboy," Benny explained. "We also like to see what it looks like to a buzzard."

"Sure," agreed Reese, but the conversation soon died.

As they rode away, Bret motioned Benny and Rusty close alongside.

"Boys," he said, "that pilot wasn't just toeing the dirt aimlessly. He was making distinct marks— three dots and three dashes. That's code for the first two letters of S O S!"

"The call for help?" Benny asked.

"Right. And I've got a hunch that Ralph Reese is in real trouble!"

CHAPTER XVII

Bandits in Tovar

BRET suddenly reined up, a calculating look in his blue eyes.

"Maybe we can still find out about Reese," he said. "Rusty, you're a top-hand detective around here. Are you game to try a little trick?"

"Sure. Just so it's not roping a ghost."

"All right, here's what you do. Run back there and beg for a short plane ride. Act just as much like an overeager kid as you know how."

"Aw, shucks!"

"Now hold your 'tater! Whether you get the plane ride or not—and you likely won't—get close to Reese and whisper to him: 'Are you in trouble? Can we help you?' And make sure what his answer is. Got it?"

"Right!" Rusty answered briskly. He whirled Chopo around and hit a high lope back to the locked gate. Wiley, Colfax, and Reese were walking slowly toward the house. From their gestures, they seemed to be arguing.

With the brash courage of boyhood, Rusty jumped off his pony and wiggled under the gate.

"Oh, Mr. Reese! Mr. Colfax!" he called. "Can I speak to you just a minute?"

Wary of going too far, Rusty slowed as the three men quickly turned and came to meet him.

"All right, kid, scram!" Wiley growled.

"I'll handle this, Wiley," Colfax said harshly. "What is it you want, boy?"

"I—I just wanted to ask Mr. Reese if he'll take me for just a short little ride in the plane. I—I've never been in a plane, and—and—" Rusty stammered.

"Afraid I can't do it, son." Reese looked at Colfax as he spoke.

"Then just show me what it looks like inside, Mr. Reese," Rusty begged.

The boy tried to edge close to the pilot, but Colfax stepped between them.

"Well, son, I might do that much." Reese smiled at Rusty.

"No!" The word rang out. "You're not hired to amuse the local kids."

Reese's face flushed at the rebuke, but he did not answer back. Colfax seized Rusty's arm and propelled him toward the gate.

"I thought we were going to be neighbors now!"

Rusty said, stubbornly making a last desperate effort to achieve Bret's scheme.

"Neighbors or not," Colfax spoke coldly, *"nobody's* got any business inside that gate. Now get out and be on your way."

Rusty jerked free of Colfax's grasp and rejoined Bret and Benny.

"Mr. Reese sounded friendly," he reported, "but that old Colfax never did let me get close to him."

"Good try, Rusty," Bret commended him.

Defeated in their purpose of getting the lowdown on Reese, the boys returned to the ranch.

Supper was waiting, and so was important news. This time, however, it was not about truck rustlers, bone diggers, or bank robbers.

"Boys," Big Jim told them, "Henry Yates phoned me from Kansas this afternoon. He wants to take delivery on three truckloads of calves that he's contracted for. Looks as if we'll have to take time out from rustler hunting to load them tomorrow. Jack Bristow and José Lopez will be over from the Box M to help. Ace is coming out, but Andy and Vic can't make it."

At dawn the Rimrock Ranch crew, including Jinx, Rusty, Ace, and the two Box M cowboys, were in the saddle. With Big Jim, Bret, and Benny, the riders numbered eight in all.

Unlike the roundup of Flying Spur's wild Mexican steers, this day's gathering of cattle would be purposely slow and leisurely. Big Jim did not have to tell his riders why. They all knew that disturbing fat cattle or "chousing," as cowboys call it, takes off weight. And in the beef business, every pound means money.

Riding by threes, Big Jim and his young cow hands spent the morning in the "wet cow" pastures, carefully combing mesa, canyon, and flat for cows with calves big enough to ship.

In some instances cows with smaller calves could be left where they were. The "cutting" or sorting at the shipping corrals would be twofold: separating the smaller calf-and-mother pairs from the others, and the calves big enough to ship from their mothers.

Big Jim was almost as proud of the new corrals on Antelope Flat as he was of his best cattle. He and Bret had designed and built them to make it easy to sort, weigh, load, and otherwise handle cattle without hurry, rough treatment, or undue excitement.

At about two o'clock in the afternoon the Rimrock Ranch crew began funneling the herd through a wide-winged gate into the big holding pen, fenced with heavy wire mesh six feet high.

There was a lot of bawling, as always with a cow-and-calf herd, but with eight riders slowly crowding them, the cattle were giving no trouble.

Then, suddenly, a gray airplane roared out of the distance and swooped low right over them. The plane banked sharply, zoomed, and roared over the corral again somewhat higher. The cattle spooked at once, and a score of them jammed together just outside the gate, broke back in a sudden surge of lunging panic.

Rusty, looking up at the plane, did not see what was happening, and the onrush of frightened cattle knocked his pony down. Suddenly Rusty found himself afoot in the midst of trampling hoofs and tossing horns!

Bret, also watching the plane, was trying to read its identification numbers. He was unaware of the accident until he heard Jinx cry out in alarm. But Big Jim had seen it, and he got there quickly. In one strong-armed swoop he lifted Rusty safely to the saddle in front of him.

Even these gentle cattle could have trampled the

boy badly, and the pallor of Big Jim's face was proof that he knew it. Yet now that his son was safe, the rancher could not restrain a prideful chuckle.

"When I got there," he told the others, "Rusty was hopping on one foot, slapping cows in the face with his hat, as big as life and twice as salty! And by golly he did look funny, waving that hat."

Chopo had made his own way out of the mix-up and started for home. By the time Ace caught and brought the pony back, Rusty was ready to climb on again.

"One ol' cow stepped on my foot is all." Rusty shrugged.

"That pilot was a fool!" Big Jim declared. "Who would do such a mean thing, anyhow?"

"I wonder." Bret frowned. "There appeared to be two men in the plane besides the pilot."

"Colfax and Dudley, maybe?" Ace said.

Bret could not be sure, and nobody had had a good look at the plane's numbers.

The Box M cowboys, meanwhile, had gathered the few scattered cattle. In a short time the herd was safely corralled, ready for sorting. With no more riding to be done, Jinx left for the ranch to see if any news had come by telephone concerning the sheriff's prisoner, Wide Mouth.

While she was gone, the steer calves were shunted into one corral, all others into another. Big Jim and Bret took turns "swinging the gate" from a platform over one end of the cutting chute. By the simple turn of a lever they controlled a gate that sorted the cattle. From there, the steers were eased onto a big scale, weighed, passed into the loading chute, and thence into the three big trailer trucks hired to haul them to Kansas.

The work was almost finished when Jinx came galloping back from the ranch. "Andy just phoned," she called out excitedly. "The Tovar bank has been held up! Sheriff Buxton was gassed and badly beaten! Andy needs help!"

"Just as Mr. Martinson feared!" Bret said. "Come on, Dad!"

Big Jim hesitated only a moment. "Benny, you and Ace supervise the loading. Bret and I will have to go."

Father and son galloped their horses to the ranch, then sped to Tovar.

Waiting for them at the bank were Andy, Vic, Mrs. Martinson, and the sheriff in street clothes with a bandage on his head.

"How did it happen?" Big Jim asked.

"I was staked out in Martinson's office," Sheriff Buxton said, "when Orvel was called to a teller's cage. I looked around at the Western paintings in the office—the way a man will when he's waiting. Suddenly a fellow in a gas mask appeared in the door with a strange-looking pistol. It made a zizzing noise."

Buxton paused briefly to collect his thoughts,

then continued. "I had purposely worn a business suit so as not to be spotted in case the crooks did show up. I reached for the gun I had in my belt, but my arm just wouldn't work right. Next thing I knew I came to with bruises all over me."

Martinson carried on the story. "Meanwhile, out in the bank, another masked man fogged the place with nerve gas, knocking out all of us, including Buxton's two deputies, who never had a chance to put on their gas masks. When I regained consciousness, the sheriff was coming out of my office, so groggy he could hardly stand. The office safe had been cleaned out, as well as all the tellers. I don't know yet how much money was stolen, but it was plenty—and the bandits are gone without a trace!"

State Police officers were now on the premises, dusting for fingerprints and checking footprints on the waxed floor. But, as in the other robberies, they could find nothing to identify the criminals.

The Kings were about to leave when a thin, wiry man hurried into the bank and went straight to Buxton.

"Hello, Paget," the sheriff said wearily. "I gave you the story for your newspaper half an hour ago."

The editor of the *Tovar Times* smiled and reached into his pocket, pulling out a sheet of paper torn from a teletype machine. "Buck, this may be the answer to the gas-gun gimmick."

The news item told about recent thefts of nerve gas from a big chemical laboratory near Denver.

"More evidence," Buxton said bitterly, "but still nothing to identify the criminals. Thanks, Russ. I'll follow up this clue."

Baffled by this latest bank robbery, Bret and Big Jim drove back to the ranch in time for supper. They were just leaving the table, discussing what to do next, when Rusty, turning from a window, exclaimed:

"Dad! Bret! Come look! A station wagon is out front—with Colfax and Dudley!"

CHAPTER XVIII

A Secret Message

DUDLEY was at the wheel. He braked the station wagon to a stop beside the vine-covered portal. Bret noticed the Pennsylvania license plate as the car swung around.

Although the station wagon was dusty and mud-spattered, the lettering on its side was easy to read: PENN'S GROVE COLLEGE was the first line, ARCHAEOLOGICAL EXPEDITION below it.

Big Jim and the boys stepped outside to meet the callers. Dudley got out of the car and came toward the porch with a friendly, disarming smile on his freshly shaved, square face. But Bret thought Colfax looked sullen and wary.

"Good evening!" Dudley addressed Big Jim pleasantly. "I'm Dr. Dudley. This is my colleague, Professor Colfax. I imagine you're a bit surprised to see us, Mr. King."

He started to offer his hand, then did not when

155

he saw that the rancher's hands stayed thumb-hooked in the pockets of his denims.

"Howdy," said Big Jim. He hesitated, but the habit of Western hospitality is strong. "Won't you come in?" he added.

"Why, thank you kindly." Dudley smiled. "A very attractive place you have here. Quite in harmony with its environment."

"Thanks," Big Jim said. "We figure it fits the country."

He held the screen door open and the two callers went in. More than a little puzzled, Big Jim, Bret, Ace, and Rusty followed.

A moment after the visitors were seated in the big ranch-style living room, Jinx and Mrs. King entered from the kitchen.

"Mr. King"—Dudley cleared his throat—"my colleague and I have come to apologize for frightening your cattle this afternoon. Our pilot is a rather eccentric fellow. He seems to enjoy buzzing, as he calls it, and we were powerless to prevent him. Of course we had no idea it would frighten the cattle so badly. In any case, we apologize most sincerely."

Big Jim sat through Dudley's speech with a politely skeptical look on his weather-tanned face. He took his time about replying.

"Dudley," he said finally, "tell your pilot that his buzzing might have got my little boy trampled and badly hurt—maybe even killed."

"Frankly," Dudley said smoothly, "I've already given Reese the devil."

"Yeah, we warned him he'd get fired if he pulled any more such razzmatazz," put in Colfax.

The man doesn't speak like a college professor, Bret thought. He had been studying Colfax's features, trying in vain to figure out what it was about the man that reminded him of someone else.

"When a man offers an apology," Big Jim said bluntly, "I've got no choice but to accept it. But let's see that it doesn't happen again. How are you getting along with your archaeological work?" he added.

"Quite well, quite well, thank you. A most interesting dig." Dudley paused, then went on in a confidential tone. "You understand, of course, that there are certain aspects of our scientific research that must remain secret."

"Secret is right!" Rusty put in. "They ran me off when I asked for a ride in their airplane!"

"That was unfortunate, young man." Dudley still sounded apologetic. "I think we can arrange to give you a ride one of these days."

"By the way," Dudley said, after a moment of awkward silence, "too bad about the bank robbery in Tovar this afternoon. The wild and woolly West, eh?"

"I hear the stick-up was pulled a little after two," Colfax put in. "Just about the time we—our pilot—was buzzing your cowpens."

"Too bad the bank president was assaulted and hurt," Dudley added. "He must be a courageous man to have resisted those thugs."

Bret was electrified by Dudley's words. Why did he think it was Martinson who had been assaulted, instead of Buxton?

The cowboy felt that a trap was about to spring on Colfax and Dudley. Bret managed to sound casual. "Where did you hear the news?"

"On the radio," Colfax replied.

Rusty opened his mouth to speak, but Bret's stealthy poke in his ribs silenced the boy. The Kings knew that the radio reports of the robbery had been correct. Colfax and Dudley could not have gotten their information from the news broadcasts. Why were they lying?

"We didn't hear the full account. Maybe you can tell us more about it," Bret said.

"We heard the report soon after our flight over the ranch," Dudley replied smoothly. "About all it said was that apparently some kind of gas was used, that the bank president was found gassed and beaten in his office, and that the bandits escaped."

In spite of their efforts to remain calm, Bret and Big Jim exchanged startled glances. Obviously the robbers had found Sheriff Buxton in Martinson's office and mistaken him for the bank president. Yet Dudley and Colfax still thought it had been Martinson.

That could mean only one of two things: *either*

Dudley and Colfax were the robbers themselves, or the bandits had communicated with them after the theft!

Bret was tempted to face them with proof of their lying here and now. Yet they had an alibi, and their pilot was a witness. Without more tangible evidence, Bret thought, what could he accomplish? Being sure of his own suspicions did not mean that the time was ripe for action. The final close-in on this sinister organization of criminals would still have to wait for red-handed evidence.

Bret was aware that Big Jim, Ace, and the others were following his lead. To break the awkward silence, he said:

"That's interesting, Dr. Dudley. "We hadn't heard about Mr. Martinson—the bank president, that is."

"Of course—" began Dudley, then stopped abruptly as Benny's high tenor voice suddenly broke into loud singing on the portal outside. The tune was the Mexican folk song "Adelita," the words in Spanish.

"It's just Benny." Bret forced a laugh. "He gets those spells every evening. You understand Spanish, I suppose, Dr. Dudley?"

Dudley shook his head. "German, yes, but not Spanish."

"Me neither," Colfax volunteered. "These crazy chili-picker songs give me a pain."

"I'll tell Benny to tone it down a little," Bret said.

He went to the door and spoke to Benny in Spanish. Whatever Benny's answer was, it sounded sassy, but he stopped singing.

"Bien hecho, compadre!" said Ace, and Bret knew what his "well done, pal" referred to. For, instead of telling Benny to be quiet, he had told him to slip out and search the Dudley-Colfax car.

Bret knew that Big Jim and Ace had understood every word of what he had told Benny. He was also sure that even his mother, Jinx, and Rusty had caught the sense of it.

Colfax was fidgeting uneasily in his chair.

"Well, friends," Dudley said, looking at his watch, "perhaps we'd better be running along now. "I'll say again, Mr. King, that we're sorry about the plane."

"Oh, you mustn't hurry away! I'll make some fresh coffee," Mrs. King said, "and I baked cookies this afternoon. It's an old Western custom, you know!"

It galled Bret that his mother had offered such hospitality to these unsavory callers, but he realized she was doing it to give Benny time to search their car.

"That's fine, Mom!" Bret said, then turned to Dudley. "My mother makes the best cookies you ever tasted, Dr. Dudley. You wait and see!"

Bret told Benny to search the station wagon

"Well"—Dudley frowned and subsided in his chair—"if you insist."

Big Jim and Ace tried to keep the conversation going and gain information from Colfax and Dudley.

"There's a story of the cliff dwellings," Ace volunteered, "that they are haunted by the ghost of a Spanish soldier with his skull split open by an Indian—maybe one of my ancestors."

"I don't suppose you've found anything like a split skull in your diggings?" Big Jim inquired.

"Our excavations have been somewhat limited thus far," Dudley replied. "But the skull story certainly is interesting. Later on perhaps—"

Another sudden outburst of song outside the window interrupted him. Once more the tune was "Adelita," but the words did not come out entirely even with the tune—and Bret knew why. Instead of "Adelita," Benny was singing a message in Spanish:

"I searched the car. In the glove compartment I found two queer-looking pistols wrapped up in a black cloth. After the men leave, come to the bunkhouse and look at them."

Just to make sure, Benny sang the message twice, then shifted to "La Cucaracha." Dudley and Colfax drank coffee and ate cookies, plainly not interested in Benny's vocal accomplishments. Dudley thanked Mrs. King for the refreshments and

Colfax said good-by. Then they went out and drove away.

The instant they were out of sight, Bret, Big Jim, Ace, and Rusty rushed to the bunkhouse. A peculiar smell tingled their nostrils when they opened the door.

"What's going on here?" Bret asked.

Then he saw Benny, sprawled on the floor. In their bunks the two Box M cowboys lay stretched out, unconscious.

CHAPTER XIX

Gun Flames

ON THE floor near Benny's hand lay what looked like an oversized water pistol. Rusty started to pick it up, but Bret stopped him. Using his pocket bandanna, Bret handled the gun almost as gingerly as he would a rattlesnake.

"Rusty," said Big Jim, "run ask your mother for some smelling salts or ammonia to bring these boys to."

"I'll get water," Ace volunteered.

Meanwhile, Bret carefully examined the strange pistol. It had a bottle-shaped barrel, tapering down to a small nozzle like that on a garden spray.

"This must be the nerve-gas gun," said Bret. "It can't be anything else."

"And here's another one on Benny's bunk shelf!" Big Jim exclaimed.

"Benny must have been trying to see how it worked—and gassed all three of them," Bret surmised. "I think the effect is supposed to wear off in a few minutes."

Just then Rusty, followed by his mother, came running back with a bottle of ammonia. Mrs. King put a few drops of ammonia on a handkerchief.

Ace stood by with a bucket of cold water while Big Jim passed the handkerchief under Benny's nose. The cowboy gasped and his round, nut-brown face contorted comically. One foot kicked, then he lay still again.

"Try the water cure, Ace," said Bret.

The Navajo dashed a dipperful in Benny's face. He sputtered and sat up.

"Well, gee my wheeze!" he exclaimed in a fuzzy voice, then added in Spanish, "Poor Benny! I think he is a ghost!"

"Not quite yet," Bret assured him. "What happened?"

By the time they had revived the two Box M cowboys, Benny felt able to talk. After admitting he had pulled the trigger by mistake, Benny added, "I found these funny *pistolas* in the glove compartment, wrapped in heavy black cloth. In the same cloth I wrapped some pieces of an old mowing machine. Maybe they won't notice the guns are gone."

"Good boy!" Bret commended him. Then he drew a deep breath, like a man getting ready to dive into deep water. "This cuts the fence for sure," he said grimly. *"Colfax and Dudley robbed —or helped rob—that bank this afternoon."*

"I reckon we ought not to have let them go," Big Jim said. "But since we did, we'd better phone Sheriff Buxton right away."

But when Bret tried to ring Tovar, the phone was dead. Apparently the lead-in wire from the main road had been cut.

"From Dudley's looks," Bret declared, "I had a hunch they knew we were on to them. This proves it. Let's roll!"

"Not by the main road," Ace cautioned. "If they cut the telephone, they also may lay a trap, like barbed wire or dynamite."

"Yes," Big Jim agreed. "We might even be ambushed!"

"Then we'll take the old logging road. It's rough, but the pickup can make it."

"Ace, you and the boys have horses saddled when we get back from Tovar," said Big Jim. "We're liable to need them."

Before they started, Bret walked off a safe distance to test the captured gas guns. He located the safety catch, pointed one of the guns at arm's length downwind, and pressed the trigger. Both the zizz and the fine spray from the nozzle were weak.

When he tried the other pistol it zizzed loudly, and spray fogged from the nozzle in such a cloud that Bret stepped back quickly in astonishment. But the breeze carried the gas away.

"One is about empty; the other is full loaded,"

Bret informed Big Jim as he took the wheel of the waiting truck.

Speed and a rough road made it a wild ride to Tovar. They found Buxton and State Policeman Sanchez in the sheriff's office.

"Why, the low-down skunks!" Buxton exclaimed, when Bret finished the story and showed him the gas guns. "That pins the bank job on Colfax and Dudley for sure."

"Except for their alibi," Bret reminded him.

"It might have been two other men in the plane," said Buxton. "We'll find out."

Then he reached into a nearby file and pulled out some papers. Sheriff Buxton had not been idle. The FBI report on Williams' fingerprints identified Wide Mouth as an ex-convict wanted in Montana for cattle theft, assault, and robbery.

"Five cattlemen's associations are offering rewards," Buxton asserted. "Now look at these shoes Evans found in Williams' brown leather war bag."

One look at the worn heels told Bret that they matched the first rustler tracks found on the Rimrock Ranch.

"This hog-ties Williams as one of the truck rustlers," Bret declared. "But we still don't know whether he's in cahoots with the bank robbers."

"We'll round up the whole shebang and get some answers," Buxton said. "I've got posse men standing by—Officer Sanchez, Bill Evans and Jenkins from the Flying Spur, and three deputies I can depend on."

"Throw in Big Jim, Bret, Ace, Benny, Vic and me, Rusty, and fifty cents' worth of rattlesnakes," drawled Andy, "and we could just about capture the whole state of Texas!"

"Who wants Texas?" Bret quipped, then added seriously, "Just the same, we're at your service, Sheriff."

"If that surprised me any I'd say so," replied Buxton dryly. "Now here's the plan: my posse will hit the Oro Perdido farther down. We'll coyote up the canyon, surround the Ortega place, and nab the whole gang—if they're there. If they're not— that's where you boys come in."

"They might get away in the plane," Bret pointed out. "In that case we'll be too late. Otherwise, they can either try to escape down the canyon—"

"We'll head 'em off there!" broke in Buxton.

"Or else," Bret went on, "there's the old road around the foot of the mesa to Rimrock headquarters, and there's the trail up to the cliff dwellings and on over the ridge."

Buxton nodded. "So I want you and your pals to block those escape routes—pronto!" He handed Bret one of the gas guns. "Maybe you'll need this."

"Sheriff," Bret said earnestly, "there's more likely to be a fight at the Ortega place."

"I know," Buxton replied. "If there's gunsmoke, you boys want to be there. Just don't be too sure you won't get your share up on the ridge."

With some reluctance Bret finally agreed. Big Jim elected to go along with the posse. This well-armed group would go as far as possible by car, then take it afoot.

Bret, Andy, and Vic were already bouncing on

the old logging road to the Rimrock Ranch by the time the sheriff got his posse together.

At the ranch Benny and Ace had horses ready. Briefly, Bret reported the plan of action. Benny complained. "Does that sheriff think we're just a bunch of kids?"

"Actually," Vic explained, "the New Mexican law does not permit the sheriff to appoint anyone under twenty-one as an official deputy carrying firearms."

"Aw, shucks!" Rusty muttered.

"Official deputies or not," Bret said, "we've got a job to do—and we'd better get going!"

When Jack Bristow and José Lopez, the Box M cowboys, offered to help, Bret accepted their company. But he ruled that Rusty would have to stay at the ranch, much to the boy's regret.

They rode by moonlight, they rode fast, and they all rode together at first. Crossing one end of a long, narrow flat, still several miles from their destination, Ace suddenly drew rein.

"Look! There in the edge of the bush!"

Approaching cautiously, the boys saw the familiar gray airplane, cleverly camouflaged with tree branches. Even more cautiously, they surrounded it. When nothing moved, they crowded around the craft. Still safely distant from the Oro Perdido, Bret felt it safe to use a flashlight. Chalked on the plane's windows were two outlines of men's heads.

"I'll be a burro's uncle!" Bret exclaimed. "That's

why I thought I saw three men when it buzzed the shipping pens!"

"Colfax and Dudley's alibi!" Vic declared. "They weren't in the plane at all."

"It would be a reasonable deduction," Bret said, "that this plane is the same craft that spied on us the day we found the wrecked truck."

"Reasonable deduction, my eye!" said Andy. "It's a plain ol' fact. But what's it doing here?"

"Probably planted for a hasty getaway," Vic suggested.

"Why don't we break a wing or something so it can't fly?" Benny suggested.

"I know easier way," Ace offered. "Take rotor out of the timer. No juice, no fly."

With the help of Vic's flashlight, Ace did not take long to remove the rotor. He put the part in his pocket. They rode on, certain now that Colfax and Dudley could not escape in the plane.

Judging that the wanted men would be least likely to try escaping in the direction of the Rimrock Ranch, Bret sent the Box M cowboys to guard that possible exit. Then Bret, Andy, Ace, Benny, and Vic turned their horses up the rough, steep climb to the ridge of the cliff dwellings.

The riders moved slowly in order to make their approach as quiet as possible. But the *clink-clank* of shod hoofs on a rocky trail could not be muffled.

Far out below and miles away, the headlights of

cars on the highway gleamed and flashed like lightning bugs. The sight gave Bret an odd feeling of farawayness—almost of loneliness, even with his companions near.

Topping the ridge where Vic had previously lost his flashlight, the boys left their horses and continued on foot toward the cliff dwellings. Except for the *put-put* of a motor, and two lighted windows in the valley, all was quiet and dark around the Ortega place.

Did it mean that the outlaws had already escaped? Bret wondered fearfully. As they reached a wall-tumbled cliff room of the ruins, Bret got his answer. Above the wind moaning over the chimney rock came the crackle of rifle fire. Orange-red gun flames blossomed below. The posse's battle had begun.

"What a fight!" Andy exclaimed. "Wish I were down there!"

"If Dad and the sheriff are winning," Bret said, "those crooks may hightail up this way. Come on, fellows."

Searching for the trail, Bret's flashlight suddenly gleamed on a blanched human skull. It was cleft through the top, as if by a sword!

"Look!" Bret gasped. "This must be the Spanish soldier Don Miguel told us about!"

As Bret reached to pick up the skull, the boys were startled by a harsh voice behind them.

"Hands up! Don't move or we'll blast you!"

CHAPTER XX

The Showdown

DUDLEY'S voice! Bret's heart pounded at the thought, while the muzzle of a gun pressed firmly against his back. As he slowly raised his hands, a light flashed on, revealing that Andy, Benny, and Vic had done the same. Only Ace stood ramrod stiff, his hands still at his sides.

"Suicide won't help, Ace," Bret advised quietly. "Better do as they say."

With deliberation that still smacked of defiance, Ace lifted his hands.

"In one more second," jeered the harsh voice of Colfax, "we'd have had us a dead Injun!"

One of Vic's high-reaching hands still held a lighted flashlight. Its beams illuminated the stone ceiling, smoke-blackened by the fires of a vanished people. Bret saw Vic's wrist start to turn the blinding glare into the eyes of the jeering Colfax. With an oath, Colfax seized the flashlight and jerked it out of Vic's hand.

"Well, cowboys," sneered Dudley, "you heard that shooting—but you don't hear it now. That was Wiley and the boys, forted up in that adobe with shotguns, rifles, and pistols, blasting your stupid sheriff and his mob. Your slowpoke posse never had a chance!"

Bret's heart felt like a lump of lead inside his chest. If Colfax's bragging were true—

"We've arranged a special program for you punks," Dudley said. "Just a few steps around the ledge is the top of one of those tall, hollow chimney rocks. We're going to drop you all right into it. Then we're taking off in our plane. We can reach another hide-out long before anybody even discovers your bodies."

Dudley paused to laugh scornfully. "Then old man Ortega will have some real ghosts to spin yarns about!"

Bret now noticed that a third man stood back in the shadows. It was Ralph Reese.

"Look here, Grote," Reese said, obviously addressing Dudley, "that would be cold-blooded murder!"

"*Mister* Reese," Dudley taunted him, "don't you want to go back to your family in one piece? I'm sure we can fix it otherwise."

"All right, Grote," Reese said quietly. "But I want these boys to understand that I'm not mixed up in this. King, when these crooks chartered my plane, I didn't know what they were up to. Then they threatened me at gun point and forced me to—"

"Shut up!" Colfax whirled and slapped the pilot across the mouth. Reese staggered backward.

For an instant Colfax's flashlight swung around, off the prisoners.

Quick as the strike of a rattlesnake, Bret dropped to his knees and threw himself sideways.

Crack! Dudley fired. The bullet passed over Bret and whined off the cliff wall.

With a bloodcurdling war whoop, Ace leaped on Colfax. In that split second of confusion, Bret's right hand ripped open his shirt, jerked out the loaded gas gun, and fired a spray of fumes directly into Dudley's face.

The criminal's surprised oath ended in a strangled cough. Grimly Bret held pressure on the trigger. How much gas it would take to do the job he had no idea, but he meant to make it enough.

In the ancient cliff room, only partly open on one side, the fog of gas thickened and took effect quickly. Before Bret realized what was happening, Dudley, Colfax, Reese, Andy, Benny, Ace, Vic, and himself all lay strewn about, as unconscious as the ancient split skull gleaming ghostly white in the glare of a dropped flashlight.

Bret did not know how long he had lain there unconscious. What he did know was that Big Jim's anxious face, looking down at him when he tried to sit up, was the most welcome sight his eyes had ever seen.

"Easy does it, son." Big Jim's voice was reassuring. "Everything's under control."

There were lots of flashlights now. In their glow Bret could see the perpetual white-toothed Ortega grin. Benny had been the first to recover.

"Well, gee my wheeze!" He indicated the handcuffs on Colfax, Dudley, and Reese. "All from a sudden we go to sleep—and somebody put hobbles on the burros."

As soon as the boys were clearheaded enough to listen, Sheriff Buxton, with a bloody bandanna wrapped around his left arm, reported on the posse's success.

"We outfoxed 'em," he said. "We tied flashlights on the ends of long sticks. Some of us approached the house, holding the lights way out to one side. While the crooks wasted time shooting at the men they thought were behind the flashlights, the rest of us snake-sneaked into the house and jumped 'em. They squealed on Colfax and Dudley and told us how to get here."

"Are you badly hurt, Sheriff?" Bret asked. "Did anyone else get shot?"

"Mine's only a meat scratch," Buxton replied. "Sanchez got nicked in the leg. Evans suffered two bullet holes in a thirty-dollar hat. Two crooks were wounded, but they'll live to go to the pen—along with these kingpins here."

"They've got a diesel generator and a huge freeze locker full of stolen beef down there," said Big Jim.

"It looks like a smart operation," Bill Evans added. "They could steal beef in one part of the country, rush it by truck or plane to a hide-out hundreds of miles away, freeze it there, and market it at their leisure."

"Pretty clever, eh, Dudley?" said Bret.

"His name isn't Dudley," said Reese. "He's Grote Grimshaw, one of the smartest criminals in the country. Did time in four states, for everything from forgery to robbery while impersonating an officer. He told me so himself."

"And now he'll do time in New Mexico," Andy said, "for trying to outfox a bunch of rawhide Rimrock riders."

"You see," Big Jim explained, "we found the real Dr. Dudley and Professor Colfax of Penn's Grove locked up in that stone hut that Don Miguel used to store wool."

"The phony Colfax's real name is Collard Williams," Reese broke in. "Wide Mouth is his brother."

"So that's what bothered me!" exclaimed Bret. "Colfax's resemblance to his brother."

"Remember Grimshaw calling him 'Col' the day

they moved in?" said Vic. " 'Col' for 'Collard,' not Colfax."

"He's collared for sure now!" Andy quipped.

"As I was saying before you boys got a head start on me," Big Jim went on, "the real archaeologists say these scoundrels struck up an acquaintance with them in an Omaha restaurant. Offered to show them some digger-Indian ruins, then kidnaped them, stole their station wagon, and borrowed their names."

"Sheriff," Bret asked, "can't we take the handcuffs off Reese? I believe he was shanghaied into all of this against his will."

"That's the truth," Reese said. "I wasn't mixed up in this. They chartered my plane and said they'd kill me unless I went along with their plans. They never let me out of their sight. I had to buzz your cattle, because one of the gang was crouched down in the plane with a gun in my ribs. And that day you saw Grimshaw getting out of the plane it was the same way."

"We thought you were in trouble," Bret said. "We wanted to help you, but there was no way."

"I should have conked you hard enough to shut your mouth for keeps!" Grimshaw snarled.

"You mean that night at Otto's?" Bret asked.

"Yeah," Grimshaw said bitterly. "Wide Mouth radioed us that you were spying. I just didn't wallop you hard enough, that's all."

"I'd like to conk that brother of mine," Collard

Williams growled. "I wanted to keep the beef and bank business separate, but he had to gum it up. So now we're up to our necks in trouble."

"Deeper than that, Collard," Buxton said dryly. "Bank robbery, rustling, that nerve gas—"

"That was Grote's smart idea," Williams complained.

"You blabbermouthed rat!" snarled Grimshaw.

"Hold it!" Buxton advised. "You'll have plenty of time to blab in court."

While the sheriff released Reese, Bret fished two little black bulls from his pocket.

"Ever see these before, Williams?"

"Why not?" Williams shrugged. "My brother Wide Mouth lost one when the truck turned over. I don't know where you got the other. That was another one of Grimshaw's trick ideas—carrying those fool bulls as a gang identification. I warned him they would get us in trouble."

"Aw, shut up and quit crying!" Grimshaw said, apparently disgusted. "We're all in this soup together."

"Where's the bank loot?" Buxton asked the prisoners.

"Find it yourself," Grimshaw snapped.

"They brought it with them," Reese offered. "It must be somewhere around here."

A search was started quickly in and around the boulders and craggy nooks. Finally Ace called out from behind a chimney rock, and pulled out a fat suitcase. The sheriff opened it and stacks of green-backs tumbled out.

"It's the stolen money all right," Buxton said.

While the posse took the prisoners to Tovar by car, Bret and the boys rode back. On the way the Box M cowboys joined them, pleased at their success.

At the ranch Mrs. King, Jinx, and Rusty were overjoyed at their safe return and proud of the Rimrock riders. So was all of Tovar.

In the sheriff's office the next day there was not much more left to thresh out. One of the prisoners proved to be the eavesdropper that Andy and Bret had aided in changing a flat tire.

When Wide Mouth learned that the gang had been rounded up, he talked freely, even with a touch of braggadocio, about his part in the plot. It had been Wide Mouth, scouting the Oro Perdido Canyon before the arrival of the rest of the mob, who had knocked out Benny. Williams also had wrecked the truck and had hidden behind the juniper branches, spying on the boys, until the airplane returned later to pick him up.

"I ain't really a cowboy," Wide Mouth said with a smirk.

"So we noticed," Bret said.

Buxton had already helped Reese report by long-distance telephone to his wife.

"There'll be a whole batch of rewards for you boys," Buxton told Bret, "along with my thanks."

With the thieves safely jailed, Big Jim and the boys returned to the ranch, taking Reese with them. That afternoon, after some broad hints from Benny and Rusty, Reese took them for a sky spin over the big ranch—after Ace replaced the rotor. Jinx, Rusty, Vic, and Andy made up the first load.

"I love it!" exclaimed Jinx when they landed. "It rides as smooth as whipped cream!"

"Gosh!" Rusty observed. "I never knew everything was so far down from up there."

"Beats dragging your feet on those midget mustangs of yours," Bret teased him, as he and Ace and Benny climbed in for their turn.

When they soared over the Sabinoso, Don Miguel and Doña Mela waved at them, having heard the good news.

Looking down on the great expanse of mesa, rimrock, canyon, and plain that he knew and loved so well, Bret suddenly exclaimed, "Boy! I'd sure like to own one of these birds myself. I'll bet I could learn to fly!"

"Of course you could," Reese said.

"The reward money!" Ace said, his black eyes gleaming. "Why not use it to buy a plane?"

"Great idea!" Bret said. "Let's do just that!"

More excitement is in store for everyone at Rimrock Ranch when Bret King flies straight into new adventure involving a marauding mountain lion and an eccentric recluse in THE SECRET OF HERMIT'S PEAK.